D1231873

THE PROOF

Also by Agota Kristof

The Notebook

THE PROOF

Agota Kristof

Translated from the French by
David Watson

Grove Weidenfeld
New York

Published by Grove Weidenfeld
A division of Grove Press, Inc.
841 Broadway
New York, New York 10003-4793

Published in Canada by General Publishing Company, Ltd.

Originally published in French in 1988 under the title *La Preuve* by Editions du Seuil, Paris.

Library of Congress Cataloging-in-Publication Data

Kristof, Agota.
[Preuve. English]
The proof / Agota Kristof ; translated from the French by David Watson.—1st American ed.
p. cm.
Translation of: La preuve.
ISBN 0-8021-1112-2
I. Title.
PQ2671.R55P7413 1991
843'.914—dc20 91-19035
CIP

Manufactured in the United States of America

Printed on acid-free paper

First American Edition 1991

1 3 5 7 9 10 8 6 4 2

THE PROOF

1

On his return to Grandmother's house, Lucas lies down by the garden gate in the shade of the bushes. He waits. An army truck pulls up in front of the border post. Some soldiers get out and lower a body wrapped in a camouflaged sheet to the ground. A sergeant comes out of the border post and gives a sign, and the soldiers open the sheet. The sergeant whistles.

"It'll be a real job identifying him! You've got to be crazy to try and cross that bitch of a border, and in broad daylight too!"

A soldier says, "You'd think people would realize it's impossible."

Another soldier says, "The people around here know that. It's the ones from elsewhere who try to get across."

The sergeant says, "Okay, let's go see the idiot across the road. Maybe he knows something."

Lucas goes into the house. He sits on the corner seat in the kitchen. He slices some bread, puts a bottle of wine and some goat's cheese on the table. There is a knock. The sergeant and a soldier come in.

Lucas says, "I was expecting you. Sit down. Have some wine and cheese."

The soldier says, "Thanks."

He takes some bread and some cheese; Lucas pours the wine.

The sergeant says, "You were expecting us. Why?"

"I heard the explosion. After explosions someone always comes to ask if I saw anyone."

"And did you see anyone?"

"No."

"As usual."

"Yes, as usual. People don't come here to tell me they intend to cross the border."

The sergeant laughs. He takes some wine and cheese.

"You might have seen someone hanging around here, or in the forest."

"I saw no one."

"If you *had* seen someone, would you say so?"

"If I told you I would, you wouldn't believe me."

The sergeant laughs again. "I sometimes wonder why they call you the idiot."

"Me too. I simply have a nervous disorder due to suffering a psychological trauma as a child during the war."

The soldier asks, "What? What did he say?"

Lucas explains, "I'm a bit funny in the head because of the air raids. It happened when I was a child."

The sergeant says, "Your cheese is very good. Thank you. Come with us."

Lucas follows them. Pointing to the body, the sergeant says, "Do you know this man? Have you seen him before?"

Lucas gazes at the mangled body of his father. "He's beyond recognition."

"You can still recognize someone from his clothes, his shoes, or even his hands or hair."

Lucas says, "All I can tell is that he's not from this town. His clothes tell you that. No one wears such elegant clothes in this town."

The sergeant says, "Thank you. We knew that much already. We aren't idiots either. I'm asking you whether you have seen him before or noticed him anywhere."

"No. Nowhere. But I see his nails have been torn out. He's been in prison."

The sergeant says, "There's no torture in our prisons. It's strange that his pockets are completely empty. Not even a photo, or a key, or wallet. Yet you'd think he'd have an identity card, maybe even a pass giving him access to the border zone."

Lucas says, "He probably got rid of them in the forest."

"I think so too. He didn't want to be identified. I wonder who he was trying to protect. If by any chance you come across something when you're out picking mushrooms, you'll bring it to us, won't you, Lucas?"

"You can count on me, sergeant."

Lucas sits down on the bench in the garden and rests his head against the white wall of the house. The sun blinds him. He shuts his eyes.

"What do I do now?"

"Same as before. Keep getting up in the morning, going to bed at night, doing what has to be done in order to live."

"It will be a long time."

"Perhaps a whole lifetime."

The sounds of the animals wake Lucas. He gets up and goes to tend the livestock. He feeds the pigs, the hens, the rabbits. He rounds up the goats by the riverbank, brings them back, milks them. He carries the milk to the kitchen. He sits down on the corner seat and stays there until nightfall. Then he gets up, leaves the house, waters the garden. There is a full moon. When he goes back to the kitchen, he eats a bit of cheese and drinks some wine. He leans out of the window and throws up. He clears the table. He goes into Grandmother's room and opens the window to air it. He sits down in front of the dressing table and looks at himself in the mirror. Later Lucas opens his bedroom door. He looks at the double bed. He closes the door and goes off into town.

The streets are deserted. Lucas walks quickly. He stops in front of an open window with a light on. It is a kitchen. A family is eating the evening meal. A mother and three children around the table. Two boys and a girl. They are eating potato broth. The father isn't there. Perhaps he is at work, or in prison, or in a camp. Or else he never came back from the war.

Lucas walks past the noisy bars where, not long ago, he would sometimes play the harmonica. He doesn't go in, he keeps on walking. He goes down the unlit alleyways behind the castle, then follows the short dark street leading to the cemetery. He stops in front of the grave of Grandfather and Grandmother.

Grandmother died last year of her second stroke. Grandfather died a long time ago. The townspeople used to say he was poisoned by his wife.

Lucas's father died today trying to cross the border, and Lucas will never see his grave.

Lucas goes back home. He climbs up into the attic with the aid of a rope. There is a straw mattress, an old army blanket, a chest. Lucas opens the chest, takes out a large school notebook, and writes a few words. He closes the notebook. He lies down on the mattress.

Over his head, lit by the moonlight shining through the gable window, the skeletons of his mother and her baby hang from a beam.

Lucas's mother and little sister were killed by a shell five years ago, a few days before the end of the war, here in the garden of Grandmother's house.

Lucas is sitting on the garden bench. His eyes are closed. A horse-drawn wagon pulls up in front of the house. The noise wakes Lucas. Joseph, the market gardener, comes into the garden. Lucas looks at him.

"What do you want, Joseph?"

"What do I want? It was market day today. I waited for you until seven o'clock."

Lucas says, "Forgive me, Joseph. I forgot what day it was. If you like we can quickly load up the produce."

"Are you joking? It's two o'clock in the afternoon. I didn't come to load up, I came to ask if you still want me to sell your produce. If not, just say so. It's all the same to me. I'm only doing it as a favor to you."

"Of course, Joseph. I simply forgot that it was market day."

"It's not just today that you forgot. You also forgot last week, and the week before."

Lucas says, "Three weeks? I didn't realize."

Joseph shakes his head. "There's something not right with you. What have you done with your fruit and vegetables for the last three weeks?"

"Nothing. But I watered the garden every day, I think."

"You think? Let's take a look."

Joseph goes behind the house into the kitchen garden. Lucas follows him. The market gardener bends over the beds and swears.

"Jesus Christ! You've let it all rot. Look at those tomatoes on the ground, those overripe beans, those yellow cucumbers and black strawberries. What, are you crazy? Ruining all this good produce! You ought to be shot! You've destroyed this year's peas, and the apricots. We might just save the potatoes and the plums. Bring me a bucket!"

Lucas brings a bucket, and Joseph begins to gather up the potatoes, and the plums which have fallen into the grass. He says to Lucas, "Fetch another bucket and gather up the rotten stuff. Perhaps your pigs will eat it. God almighty! Your animals!"

Joseph rushes down to the farmyard. Lucas follows him. Joseph wipes his brow and says, "Thank God they're still alive. Give me a pitchfork so I can clean them out a bit. By what miracle did you remember the animals?"

"They don't let you forget. They cry out as soon as they're hungry."

Joseph works for several hours. Lucas helps him, following his orders. When the sun sets they go into the kitchen.

Joseph says, "For the love of God! I've never smelled such a stink! What on earth is it?" He looks around and notices a large bowl full of goat's milk. "The milk has turned. Take it out of here and throw it in the river."

Lucas obeys. When he comes back, Joseph has already aired the kitchen and washed down the tiles. Lucas goes down into the cellar and comes back with a bottle of wine and some bacon.

Joseph says, "We'll need some bread with that."

"I haven't got any."

Joseph gets up without a word and fetches a loaf of bread from his wagon.

"Here. I bought some after the market. We don't make our own anymore."

Joseph eats and drinks. He asks, "You aren't drinking? You're not eating either. What's wrong with you, Lucas?"

"I'm tired. I can't eat."

"Your face is pale beneath your tan. You're all skin and bones."

"It's nothing. It will pass."

Joseph says, "I suspected there was something bothering you. It must be a girl."

"No, it's not a girl."

Joseph winks at him. "Sure, I know what it's like to be young. But I'd be sorry to see a fine boy like you let himself go because of a girl."

"It's not because of a girl."

"What is it, then?"

"I don't know."

"You don't know? In that case you should go and see a doctor."

"Don't worry about me, Joseph. It'll pass."

"It'll pass, it'll pass. He neglects his garden, he lets the milk turn sour, he doesn't eat, he doesn't drink, and he thinks he can go on like that."

Lucas doesn't answer.

On his way out Joseph says, "Listen, Lucas. So you won't forget market day again, I'll get up an hour earlier, I'll come and wake you, and we can both load up the fruit, vegetables, and any animals you want to sell. Is that all right by you?"

"Yes. Thank you, Joseph."

Lucas gives Joseph another bottle of wine and accompanies him to his wagon.

As he whips the horse, Joseph shouts, "Take care, Lucas! Love can be fatal!"

Lucas is sitting on the garden bench. His eyes are closed. When he opens them again, he sees a little girl swinging on a branch of the cherry tree.

Lucas asks, "What are you doing there? Who are you?"

The little girl jumps to the ground. She fiddles with the pink ribbons on the ends of her braids. "Aunt Leonie wants you to go to the priest's house. He is all alone because Aunt Leonie can't work anymore. She's in bed at home, she won't get up again, she's too old. My mother doesn't have time to go to the priest's house, because she works at the factory like my father."

Lucas says, "I see. How old are you?"

"I don't know exactly. The last time it was my birthday I was five, but that was in the winter. Now it's already autumn, and I could go to school if I hadn't been born too late."

"It's already autumn?"

The little girl laughs.

"Didn't you know? It's been autumn for two days now, even though people think it's still summer because it's so warm."

"You know a lot!"

"Yes. My big brother teaches me everything. He's called Simon."

"And what are you called?"

"Agnes."

"That's a nice name."

"So is Lucas. I know you're Lucas because my aunt said, 'Go and fetch Lucas. He lives in the last house, opposite the border posts.' "

"Didn't the guards stop you?"

"They didn't see me. I went around the back."

Lucas says, "I'd like to have a little sister like you."

"Don't you have one?"

"No. If I had one I'd make her a swing. Do you want me to make you a swing?"

Agnes says, "I've got one at home, but I like to swing on other things better. It's more fun."

She jumps up, grabs the branch of the cherry tree, and swings on it, laughing.

Lucas asks, "Aren't you ever sad?"

"No, because one thing always makes up for another."

She jumps to the ground.

"You have to hurry to the priest's house. My aunt told me to tell you yesterday and the day before, and the day before that, but I forgot every day. She will scold me."

Lucas says, "Don't worry. I'll go this evening."

"Good. So now I'll go home."

"Stay awhile longer. Would you like to listen to some music?"

"What kind of music?"

"You'll see. Come."

Lucas takes the little girl in his arms. He goes into his room, puts the child down on the double bed, and puts a record on the old gramophone. Sitting on the ground next to the bed, his head resting on his arms, he listens.

Agnes asks, "Are you crying?"

Lucas shakes his head.

She says, "I'm scared. I don't like this music."

Lucas takes one of the little girl's legs in his hand. He squeezes it. She cries out, "You're hurting me! Let me go!"

Lucas loosens his grip.

When the record finishes, Lucas gets up to turn it over. The little girl has disappeared. Lucas listens to records until sunset.

That evening Lucas makes up a basket of vegetables, potatoes, eggs, cheese. He kills a chicken and cleans it. He also takes milk and a bottle of wine.

He rings the bell of the priest's house. No one answers. He goes in through the unlocked back door and puts the basket down in the kitchen. He knocks on the bedroom door. He goes in.

The priest, a tall, thin, old man, is sitting at his desk. He is playing chess, alone, by the light of a candle.

Lucas pulls up a chair, sits facing the priest, and says, "I'm sorry, Father."

The priest says, "I'll repay you a bit at a time for what I owe you, Lucas."

Lucas asks, "Have I not been here for a long time?"

"Not since the beginning of the summer. Don't you remember?"

"No. Who has been feeding you all this time?"

"Leonie has been bringing me a little soup each day. But she has been ill for the last few days."

Lucas says, "Forgive me, Father."

"Forgive you? For what? I haven't paid you in months. I have no money left. The State has broken links with the Church, and I am no longer paid for my work. I have to live off the donations of my flock. But people stay away from church for fear of disapproval. Only a few poor old women come to mass."

Lucas says, "If I didn't come, it wasn't because of the money you owe me. It's worse than that."

"What do you mean, 'worse than that'?"

Lucas lowers his head. "I completely forgot about you. I also forgot about my garden, the market, the milk, the cheese. I even forgot to eat. For months I've been sleeping in the attic. I was afraid to go into my room. It was only because a little girl, Leonie's niece, came today that I had the courage to go in. She also reminded me of my duty toward you."

"You have no duty, no obligation toward me. You sell your produce, you live from the proceeds. If I can't pay you it's right that you not supply me anymore."

"As I said, it's not because of the money. Try to understand."

"Tell me. I'm listening."

"I don't know how to go on living."

The priest gets up, takes Lucas's face in his hands. "What has happened to you, my child?"

Lucas shakes his head. "I can't explain. It's like an illness."

"I see. A sort of illness of the soul. Due to your tender age and, perhaps, your excessive solitude."

Lucas says, "Maybe. I will make a meal and we will eat together. I haven't eaten for a long time, either. When I try to eat, I just vomit. With you I might be able to manage it."

He goes to the kitchen, lights the fire, boils up the chicken with the vegetables. He sets the table, opens a bottle of wine.

The priest comes into the kitchen.

"As I said, Lucas, I can't pay you anymore."

"Nevertheless, you have to eat."

"Yes, but I don't need this banquet. A few potatoes and some corn would be enough."

Lucas says, "You will eat what I bring you, and we won't talk anymore about money."

"I can't accept."

"It is easier to give than to receive, is that it? Pride is a sin, Father."

They eat in silence. They drink wine. Lucas doesn't vomit. After the meal he does the washing up. The priest goes back into his room. Lucas joins him.

"I have to go now."

"Where are you going?"

"To walk around the streets."

"I could teach you to play chess."

Lucas says, "I don't think I could get interested. It's a complicated game that requires a lot of concentration."

"Let's try."

The priest explains the rules. They play a game. Lucas wins. The priest asks, "Where did you learn to play chess?"

"From books. But this is the first real game I've played."

"Will you play again sometime?"

Lucas comes every evening. The priest improves his strategies, and the games become interesting, even though Lucas always wins.

Lucas starts sleeping in his bedroom again, on the double bed. He doesn't forget market days, he doesn't let the milk go sour. He takes care of the animals, the garden, the house. He goes back into the forest to collect mushrooms and firewood. He takes up fishing again.

When he was a child, Lucas caught fish by hand or with a rod. Now he invents a system that diverts the fish from the mainstream into a pool where they are trapped. Then Lucas only needs to scoop them out in a net when he wants fresh fish.

In the evenings Lucas eats with the priest, plays a game or two of chess, then walks around the streets of the town.

One night he goes into the first bar he meets on his way. It used to be a well-kept café, even during the war. Now it is a dingy place, almost empty.

An ugly, weary waitress shouts from the counter, "How many?"

"Three."

Lucas sits at a table stained with red wine and cigarette ash. The waitress brings him three glasses of cheap red wine. She collects his money right away.

When he has finished his three glasses, Lucas gets up and leaves. He pushes on as far as the main square. He stops in front of the book and stationery store and stands gazing into the window: school notebooks, pencils, erasers, and a few books.

Lucas goes into the bar opposite.

It is a bit livelier, but it is even dirtier than the other bar. The floor is covered with sawdust.

Lucas sits next to the open door, the only form of ventilation in the place.

A group of border guards are sitting around a long table. They have girls with them. They are singing.

A ragged little old man comes and sits at Lucas's table.

"How about playing something, eh?"

Lucas shouts, "A half bottle and two glasses!"

The little old man says, "I wasn't scrounging a drink, I just wanted you to play. Like before."

"I can't play like before."

"I know. But play anyway. I'd like that."

Lucas pours the wine. "Drink."

He takes his harmonica out of his pocket and starts to play a sad song, a song about love and separation.

The border guards and the girls take up the tune. One of the girls comes and sits next to Lucas; she strokes his hair.

"Isn't he cute?"

Lucas stops playing. He gets up.

The girl laughs. "Touchy!"

Outside it is raining. Lucas goes into a third bar, orders another three glasses. When he starts playing, the customers' eyes turn to him, then back to their drinks. People come here to drink, not talk.

Suddenly, a large, well-built man, with one leg amputated, plants himself on his crutches in the middle of the room beneath the single bare light bulb and begins to sing a forbidden song. Lucas accompanies him on the harmonica.

The other customers drink up quickly, and one after another leave the bar.

Tears run down the man's cheeks as he sings the last two lines of the song:

The people have already atoned
For the past and the future.

The next day Lucas goes to the book and stationery shop. He picks out three pencils, a pack of lined paper, and a thick notebook. When he comes to the cash register, the bookseller, a pale, obese man, says to him, "I haven't seen you for a long time. Have you been away?"

"No. I was just too busy."

"Your consumption of paper is most impressive. I sometimes wonder what it is you do with it."

Lucas says, "I like filling up blank sheets with pencil. It passes the time."

"You must have a mountain of them by now."

"I waste a lot. I use the spoiled pages to light the fire."

The bookseller says, "Unfortunately my other customers aren't as regular as you. Business is poor. Before the war, things were good. There were lots of schools around here. High schools, boarding schools, secondary schools. The students wandered through the streets in the evening having fun. There was also a musical conservatory, concerts and plays every week. Look out there now. Nothing but children and old people. A few workers, a few winegrowers. There are no more young people in this town. The schools have been moved to the interior of the country, all except the primary school. The young people, even those who aren't studying, move away, to towns that have some life. Our town is dead, empty. The border zone, sealed off, forgotten. Everyone knows everyone else in this town. Always the same faces. No outsiders can get in."

Lucas says, "There are the border guards. They're young."

"Yes, poor fellows. Locked away in their barracks, on patrol at night. Every six months they change them to keep them from forming contacts with the townspeople. This town has ten thousand inhabitants, plus three thousand foreign soldiers and two thousand of our own border guards. Before the war there were five thousand students, and tourists during the summer. The tourists came from the interior as well as from across the border."

Lucas asks, "The border was open?"

"Of course. The farmers from over there came to sell their produce here, the students went to the other side for village fairs. The train used to run to the next big town in the other country.

Now this town is the end of the line. Everybody off! And show your papers!"

Lucas asks, "You could come and go freely? You could travel abroad?"

"Of course. You've never known what that's like. Now you can't take a step without having to show your identity card. And the special permit for the border zone."

"What if you haven't got one?"

"It's better to have one."

"I haven't got one."

"How old are you?"

"Fifteen."

"You should have one. Even children get an identity card at school. What do you do when you leave town and then come back?"

"I never leave town."

"Never? You don't even go to the next town when you need to buy something you can't find here?"

"No. I haven't left this town since my mother brought me here six years ago."

The bookseller says, "If you want to avoid trouble, get yourself an identity card. Go to the town hall and explain your case. If anyone gives you trouble, ask for Peter N. Tell him Victor sent you. Peter comes from the same town as me. Up north. He has an important position in the Party."

Lucas says, "That's kind of you. But why should I have problems getting an identity card?"

"You never know."

* * *

Lucas goes into a large building near the castle. Flags hang from the facade. Numerous black plaques with gold lettering indicate the offices:

POLITICAL BUREAU OF THE REVOLUTIONARY PARTY
SECRETARIAT OF THE REVOLUTIONARY PARTY
ASSOCIATION OF REVOLUTIONARY YOUTH
ASSOCIATION OF REVOLUTIONARY WOMEN
FEDERATION OF REVOLUTIONARY TRADE UNIONS

Through the door a simple gray plaque with red letters:

COUNCIL INQUIRIES SECOND FLOOR

Lucas goes up to the second floor, knocks on a frosted window above which is written: "Identity cards."

A man in gray overalls opens the sliding window and looks at Lucas without speaking.

Lucas says, "Hello. I'd like to apply for an identity card."

"Renew, you mean. Your present one's expired?"

"No, I don't have one. I've never had one. Someone told me I'm supposed to have one."

The official asks, "How old are you?"

"Fifteen."

"Then you are supposed to have one. Give me your school card."

Lucas says, "I haven't got a card. Of any kind."

The official says, "That's not possible. If you are still at primary school you have your school card; if you are a student you have your student card; if you are an apprentice you have your apprenticeship card."

Lucas says, "I'm sorry. I haven't got any of those. I never went to school."

"How come? School is compulsory up to the age of fourteen."

"I was excused from school because of a psychological disorder."

"So what are you doing now?"

"I live off the produce from my garden. I also play music in bars at night."

The official says, "Ah, it's you. Lucas T., is that your name?"

"Yes."

"Who do you live with?"

"I live in Grandmother's house near the border. I live alone. Grandmother died last year."

The official scratches his head. "Listen, you're a special case. I'll have to check on this. I can't decide this on my own. You'll have to come back in a few days."

Lucas says, "Peter N. might be able to straighten it out."

"Peter N.? The Party Secretary? You know him?" He picks up the telephone.

Lucas tells him, "I was recommended by Victor."

The official hangs up and comes out of his office.

"Come on. We're going downstairs."

He knocks on a door marked SECRETARIAT OF THE REVOLUTIONARY PARTY. They go in. A young man is sitting behind a desk. The official hands him a blank card.

"It's about an identity card."

"I'll take care of it. Leave us."

The official leaves. The young man gets up and offers his hand to Lucas.

"Hello, Lucas."

"You know me?"

"Everyone in town knows you. I'm very pleased to be of service to you. Let's fill in your card. Last name, first name, address, date of birth. You're only fifteen? You're big for your age. Occupation? Shall I write 'musician'?"

Lucas says, "I also live off the produce from my garden."

"Then I'll write 'gardener.' It looks more responsible. Now let's see, brown hair, gray eyes . . . political allegiance?"

Lucas says, "Cross that out."

"All right. And here, what do you want me to write here—'Official assessment'?"

" 'Idiot,' if possible. I suffered a traumatic disorder. I'm not quite normal."

The young man laughs. "Not quite normal? Who would believe it? But you're right. An assessment like that could spare you a lot of inconvenience. Military service, for example. I'll write 'chronic psychological problems.' Does that suit you?"

Lucas says, "Yes, sir. Thank you, sir."

"Call me Peter."

Lucas says, "Thank you, Peter."

Peter comes close to Lucas and hands him his card. With his other hand he gently touches Lucas's face. Lucas closes his eyes. Peter kisses him lingeringly on the mouth, holding Lucas's head in his hands. He stays looking at Lucas's face for a moment, then he sits down at his desk.

"Excuse me, Lucas. I was moved by your beauty. I must be very careful. The Party does not forgive this sort of thing."

Lucas says, "No one will know about it."

Peter says, "You can't hide such a vice all your life. I won't stay long in this post. I'm only here because I deserted, gave myself up, and returned with the victorious army of our liberators. I was still a student when I was sent off to war."

Lucas says, "You should get married, or at least have a mistress to allay suspicion. You should find it easy to attract a woman. You are handsome, masculine. And you are sad. Women like sad men. What's more, you have a good position."

Peter laughs. "I have no desire to attract a woman."

Lucas says, "Nevertheless, there are perhaps women one can love, in some way."

"You know a lot for someone your age, Lucas!"

"I don't know anything. I'm just guessing."

"If you need anything at all, come and see me."

2

It is the final day of the year. A great cold from the north has gripped the earth.

Lucas goes down to the river. He will take some fish to the priest for the New Year's Eve supper.

It is already dark. Lucas is armed with a hurricane lamp and a pickax. He starts to break the ice covering the pool. Then he hears a child crying. He points his lamp in the direction of the sound.

A woman is sitting on the little bridge that Lucas built many years ago. The woman is wrapped in a blanket. She is watching the river bearing away blocks of snow and ice. Inside the blanket a baby is crying.

Lucas approaches and asks the woman, "Who are you? What are you doing here?"

She doesn't answer. Her large, black eyes stare into the light of the lamp.

Lucas says, "Come."

He wraps his right arm around her. He guides her toward the house, lighting the way ahead. The child is still crying.

In the kitchen it is warm. The woman sits down, uncovers her breast, and suckles the baby.

Lucas turns away. He warms up the remains of some vegetable soup.

The child sleeps on his mother's knee. The mother looks at Lucas.

"I wanted to drown him. I couldn't do it."

Lucas asks, "Do you want me to do it?"

"Do you think you could do it?"

"I've drowned mice, cats, puppies."

"A baby is a different matter."

"Do you want me to drown him or not?"

"No, not anymore. It's too late."

After a silence, Lucas says, "There's a spare room here. You can sleep here with your child."

She raises her dark eyes to Lucas. "Thank you. My name is Yasmine."

Lucas opens the door of Grandmother's room.

"Lay your child on the bed. We can leave the door open to warm the room. When you've eaten you can go and sleep next to him."

Yasmine places her child on Grandmother's bed. She comes back to the kitchen.

Lucas asks, "Are you hungry?"

"I haven't eaten since yesterday evening."

Lucas pours the soup into a bowl.

"Eat, then go to sleep. We'll talk tomorrow. I have to go now."

He goes back to the pool, scoops out two fish with the net, and goes off to the priest's house.

He prepares the meal as usual. He eats with the priest and they play a game of chess. Lucas loses for the first time.

The priest is cross.

"You are distracted this evening, Lucas. You're making stupid mistakes. Let's play again, and concentrate this time."

Lucas says, "I'm tired. I have to go home."

"You're going to hang around in the bars again."

"You are well informed, Father."

The priest laughs. "I see many old women. They tell me everything that happens in town. Don't make a face! Go on, enjoy yourself. It's New Year's Eve."

"I wish you a Happy New Year, Father."

The priest gets up, too; he places his hand on Lucas's head. "God bless you. May His peace be with you."

Lucas says, "I'll never have peace within me."

"You must pray and hope, my child."

Lucas walks down the street. He goes past the noisy bars, doesn't stop, quickens his step. When he reaches the unlit lane that leads to Grandmother's house he is running.

He opens the kitchen door. Yasmine is still sitting on the corner seat. She has opened the door of the stove; she is looking into the fire. The bowl, full of cold soup, still stands on the table.

Lucas sits down opposite Yasmine.

"You haven't eaten."

"I'm not hungry. I'm still frozen."

Lucas takes a bottle of brandy from the shelf, pours out two glasses.

"Drink. It'll warm you up inside."

He drinks, and so does Yasmine. He pours again. They drink in silence. They hear the town bells ringing in the distance.

Lucas says, "It's midnight. A new year begins."

Yasmine lowers her head onto the table. She cries.

Lucas gets up, removes the blanket which is still wrapped round Yasmine. He strokes her long, shiny black hair. He strokes her breasts, which are swollen with milk. He unfastens her blouse, bends forward, and drinks her milk.

The next day Lucas goes into the kitchen. Yasmine is sitting on the bench with the baby on her knee.

She says, "I'd like to bathe my baby. After that I'll leave."

"Where would you go?"

"I don't know. I can't stay in this town after what has happened."

Lucas asks, "What has happened? Is it the child? There are other unmarried mothers in the town. Have your parents disowned you?"

"I haven't got any parents. My mother died giving birth to me. I lived with my father and with my aunt, my mother's sister. My aunt brought me up. When my father returned from the war he married her. But he didn't love her. He only loved me."

Lucas says, "I see."

"Yes. And when my aunt found out she denounced us. My father is in prison. I worked in the hospital as a cleaner until the birth. I left the hospital this morning. I knocked at the door of our house. My aunt wouldn't open it to me. She cursed me through the door."

Lucas says, "I know your story. I've heard the gossip in the bars."

"Yes, everyone talks about it. It's a small town. I can't stay here. I was going to drown the child, then go over the border."

"You can't cross the border. You'd step on a mine."

"I don't care if I die."

"How old are you?"

"Eighteen."

"You're too young to die. You could rebuild your life somewhere else. In another town, later, when your child has grown up. For now you can stay here as long as you want."

She says, "What about the people in town?"

"They'll stop gossiping. They'll shut up eventually. You don't have to face them. We're not in the town here. This is my home."

"You would keep me here with my child?"

"You can live in this room, you can use the kitchen, but you must never go into my room or up into the attic. You must never ask me any questions."

"I won't ask you any questions and I won't disturb you. I won't let the child disturb you either. I'll cook and clean up. I can do everything. At home I did the housework, because my aunt works in a factory."

Lucas says, "The water is boiling. You can prepare the bath."

Yasmine puts a basin on the table. She takes off the child's clothes and diaper. Lucas warms a bath towel over the stove. Yasmine washes the child. Lucas watches her.

He says, "He is deformed around the shoulders."

"Yes. His legs, too. They told me at the hospital. It's my fault. I wore a tight corset around my stomach to hide the pregnancy. He'll be crippled. If only I'd had the courage to drown him."

Lucas takes the bundle in his arms, looks at the little crumpled face.

"You shouldn't say things like that, Yasmine."

She says, "He will be unhappy."

"You are unhappy yourself, yet you are not crippled. He may not be any more unhappy than you, or anyone else."

Yasmine takes back the child, her eyes filling with tears.

"You are kind, Lucas."

"You know my name?"

"Everyone knows you in town. They say you're an idiot, but I don't believe that."

Lucas goes out. He comes back with some planks of wood.

"I'm going to build him a cradle."

Yasmine does the washing, prepares the meal. When the cradle is finished, they lay the child inside. They rock him.

Lucas asks, "What is he called? Have you given him a name yet?"

"Yes. At the hospital they needed one for the town hall records. I called him Mathias. It's my father's name. I couldn't think of another name."

"You loved him that much?"

"He was all I had."

That evening Lucas comes home from the priest's house without stopping at a bar. The fire is still alight in the stove. Through the open door Lucas hears Yasmine singing softly. He goes into Grandmother's room. Yasmine, in her chemise, is rocking the child near the window.

Lucas asks, "Why aren't you in bed yet?"

"I was waiting for you."

"You don't have to wait up for me. Usually I come home a lot later."

Yasmine smiles. "I know. You play in the bars."

Lucas approaches her. He asks, "Is he asleep?"

"For a long time. I just enjoy rocking him."

Lucas says, "Come to the kitchen. We don't want to wake him."

They sit opposite each other in the kitchen, drinking brandy in silence. Later, Lucas asks, "When did it start? Between your father and you?"

"Right away. As soon as he came back."

"How old were you?"

"Twelve."

"Did he rape you?"

Yasmine laughs. "Oh no! He didn't rape me. He just lay down beside me, held me against him, kissed me, stroked me, cried."

"Where was your aunt all this time?"

"Working at the factory, on shift work. When she worked the night shift my father slept with me in my bed. It was a narrow bed in a tiny room without a window. We were happy, the two of us, in that bed."

Lucas pours some brandy. He says, "Go on."

"I grew up. My father touched my breasts. He said, 'Soon you'll be a woman, you'll go off with some boy.' I said, 'No, I'll never leave.' One night, in my sleep, I took his hand and placed it between my legs. I squeezed his fingers and felt that pleasure for the first time. The following evening it was I who asked him to give me that wonderfully sweet pleasure again. He cried, he said he musn't, that it was wrong, but I insisted, I pleaded. So he leaned over my sex, he licked it, he sucked it, he kissed it, and I felt an even more intense pleasure than the first time.

"One evening he lay on top of me, he put his sex between my thighs. He said, 'Close your legs, close them tight, don't let me enter, I don't want to hurt you.'

"For years we made love this way, but one night I couldn't resist anymore. My desire for him was too strong. I spread my legs, I was completely open, he entered me."

She stops talking. She looks at Lucas, her large dark eyes shining, her fleshy lips parted. She uncovers a breast and asks, "Do you want to?"

Lucas grabs her by the hair, drags her into the bedroom, throws her onto Grandmother's bed, and bites her neck as he takes her.

During the following days Lucas goes back to the bars. He starts walking again through the empty streets of the town.

When he gets home, he goes straight to his room.

One evening, however, coming home drunk, he opens the door of Grandmother's room. It is illuminated by the light from the kitchen. Yasmine is asleep, as is the child.

Lucas undresses and climbs into Yasmine's bed. Yasmine's body is burning, Lucas's is frozen. She is facing the wall. He presses against her back, puts his sex between Yasmine's thighs.

She closes her thighs, she moans.

"Father, oh father!"

Lucas whispers in her ear, "Tighter. Grip tighter."

She struggles, she has trouble breathing. He penetrates her. She screams.

Lucas puts his hand over Yasmine's mouth, pulls the pillow over her head. "Be quiet. You'll wake the baby!"

She bites his fingers, sucks his thumb.

When it's over, they lie there for a few minutes, then Lucas gets up.

Yasmine cries.

Lucas goes into his room.

It is summer. The child is everywhere. In Grandmother's room, in the kitchen, in the garden. He crawls around on all fours.

He is hunchbacked, deformed. His legs are too thin, his arms too long, his body ill-proportioned.

He also comes into Lucas's room. He beats on the door with his little fists until Lucas opens it. He climbs onto the bed.

Lucas puts a record on the gramophone and the child rocks on the bed.

Lucas puts on another record and the child hides under the covers.

Lucas picks up a piece of paper, draws a rabbit, a chicken, a pig. The child laughs and kisses the paper.

Lucas draws a giraffe and an elephant. The child shakes his head and tears up the paper.

Lucas constructs a sandpit for the child. He buys him a spade, a watering can, and a wheelbarrow.

He makes him a swing. He builds him a car from a box and some wheels. He sits the child in the box and pulls him around. He shows him the fish. He lets him go inside the rabbit hutch. The child tries to stroke the rabbits, but the rabbits run off crazily in all directions.

The child cries.

Lucas goes into town and buys a teddy bear.

The child looks at the bear. He takes it, talks to it, shakes it, and throws it at Lucas's feet.

Yasmine picks up the bear. She strokes it. "He's a nice bear. He's a lovely little teddy bear."

The child looks at his mother and bangs his head against the floor of the kitchen. Yasmine puts the bear down and takes the child in her arms. The child starts bawling. He pummels his mother's head and kicks her in the stomach. Yasmine lets him down, and the child hides under the table until evening.

That evening, Lucas brings back a tiny kitten he has saved

from Joseph's pitchfork. Standing on the kitchen floor, the little animal mews and trembles all over.

Yasmine places a bowl of milk in front of it. The cat continues mewing.

Yasmine places the cat in the child's cradle.

The child climbs into his cradle, lies down next to the little cat, cuddles up to it. The cat struggles and claws the child on the face and hands.

A few days later, the cat eats everything it is given and sleeps in the cradle at the child's feet.

Lucas asks Joseph to get him a little dog.

One day, Joseph turns up with a black puppy with long curly hair. Yasmine is hanging out the washing in the garden; the child is having a nap. Yasmine knocks on Lucas's door. She shouts, "Someone to see you!"

She hides in Grandmother's room.

Lucas goes out to meet Joseph. Joseph says, "Here's the dog I promised you. It's a sheepdog from the plains. It'll be a good guard dog."

Lucas says, "Thank you, Joseph. Come in and have a glass of wine."

They go into the kitchen; they drink some wine. Joseph asks, "Won't you introduce me to your wife?"

Lucas says, "Yasmine is not my wife. She had nowhere to go, so I took her in."

Joseph says, "The whole town knows her story. She's a fine-looking girl. The puppy is for her child, I presume."

"Yes, for Yasmine's child."

Before leaving, Joseph says, "You're very young to be taking care of a woman and a child, Lucas. It's a big responsibility."

Lucas says, "That's my business."

Once Joseph has gone, Yasmine comes out. Lucas is holding the little dog in his arms.

"Look what Joseph brought for Mathias."

Yasmine says, "He saw me. Did he say anything?"

"Yes. He thinks you're very beautiful. You're wrong to worry about what people might think about us, Yasmine. You should come with me into town one day to buy yourself some clothes. You've been wearing the same dress since you got here."

"One dress is enough. I don't need another one. I won't go into town."

Lucas says, "Come on, let's show Mathias the dog."

The child is underneath the kitchen table with the cat.

Yasmine says, "Mathi, it's for you. It's a present."

Lucas sits on the corner seat with the dog. The child climbs onto his knees. He looks at the dog, pulls back the hair covering its muzzle. The dog licks the child's face. The cat hisses at the dog and runs away into the garden.

It is getting progressively colder. Lucas says to Yasmine, "Mathias needs warm clothes. So do you."

Yasmine says, "I can knit. I'll need some wool and some needles."

Lucas buys a basket of balls of wool and several pairs of needles for knitting different thicknesses. Yasmine knits pullovers, socks, scarves, gloves, hats. With the leftover wool she makes up patchwork blankets. Lucas praises her.

Yasmine says, "I can also sew. At home I had my mother's old sewing machine."

"Do you want me to go and fetch it?"

"You'd be brave enough to go to my aunt's house?"

Lucas sets off with the wheelbarrow. He knocks at the door of Yasmine's aunt. A youthful-looking woman comes to the door.

"What do you want?"

"I've come to collect Yasmine's sewing machine."

She says, "Come in."

Lucas goes into a very clean kitchen. Yasmine's aunt stares at him.

"So you're the one. Poor boy. You're only a child."

Lucas says, "I'm seventeen."

"And she will soon be nineteen. How is she?"

"Well."

"And the child?"

"Also very well."

After a silence she says, "I heard that the child was born deformed. It is God's punishment."

Lucas asks, "Where is the sewing machine?"

The aunt opens a door to a narrow room without a window.

"Everything that belongs to her is here. Take it."

There is a sewing machine and a wicker basket. Lucas asks, "There was nothing else here?"

"Her bed. I burned it."

Lucas carries the sewing machine and the basket to the wheelbarrow. He says, "Thank you, madame."

"You're welcome. Good riddance."

It rains a lot. Yasmine sews and knits. The child has to play indoors. He spends the day under the table with the dog and the cat.

The child can already say a few words, but he can't walk yet. When Lucas tries to stand him upright, he struggles free, crawls away on all fours, and escapes under the table.

Lucas goes to the bookseller's. He picks out some large sheets of white paper, some colored pencils, and some picture books.

Victor asks, "You have a child?"

"Yes. But he's not mine."

Victor says, "There are so many orphans. Peter was asking after you. You should go and see him."

Lucas says, "I'm very busy."

"I understand. With a child. At your age."

Lucas goes home. The child is asleep on a rug under the kitchen table. In Grandmother's room Yasmine is sewing. Lucas puts the packet down next to the child. He goes into the bedroom and kisses Yasmine on the neck, and Yasmine stops sewing.

The child draws. He draws the dog and the cat. He also draws other animals. He draws trees, flowers, the house. He also draws his mother.

Lucas asks him, "Why don't you ever draw me?"

The child shakes his head and hides under the table with his books.

On Christmas Eve, Lucas chops down a Christmas tree in the forest. He buys some colored glass balls and some candles. In Grandmother's room he decorates the tree with Yasmine's help. The presents go under the tree: material and a pair of warm boots for Yasmine, a thick sweater for Lucas, books and a rocking horse for Mathias.

Yasmine roasts a duck in the oven. She cooks potatoes, cabbage, beans. The biscuits were made some days ago.

When the first star appears in the sky, Lucas lights the candles on the tree. Yasmine comes into the room with Mathias in her arms.

Lucas says, "Go and get your presents, Mathias. The books and the horse are for you."

The child says, "I want the horse. He's nice, the horse."

He tries unsuccessfully to climb on the horse's back. He cries.

"The horse is too big. Lucas did it. He's a nasty Lucas. He made the horse too big for Mathi."

The child cries and bangs his head against the floor of the bedroom. Lucas picks him up; he shakes him.

"The horse isn't too big. It's Mathias who is too small because he won't stand up. Always on all fours like an animal! You're not an animal!"

He is holding the child's chin to force him to look into his eyes. He says firmly, "If you don't walk now you will never walk. Never, do you understand?"

The child starts bawling. Yasmine grabs him from Lucas.

"Leave him alone! He'll walk soon enough."

She sits the child on the horse's back. She holds him upright.

Lucas says, "I have to go. Put the child to bed and wait for me. I won't be long."

He goes into the kitchen. He cuts the roast duck in two, puts half on a warm plate, surrounds it with vegetables and potatoes, and wraps the plate in a cloth. The meal is still warm when he arrives at the priest's house.

After they have eaten, Lucas says, "I'm sorry, Father, I have to go home. I'm expected."

The priest says, "I know, my son. To be honest, I'm surprised you came this evening. I know that you live in sin with a sinful woman, and with the fruit of her immoral love. That child isn't even baptized, although he bears the name of one of our saints."

Lucas is silent.

The priest says, "Come to mass, both of you, if only for this evening."

Lucas says, "We can't leave the child alone."

"Then come yourself."

Lucas says, "You're talking down to me, Father."

"Forgive me, Lucas. I was carried away by my anger. But it's because I think of you as my own son, and I fear for your immortal soul."

Lucas says, "Treat me as your son, Father. It pleases me. But you know very well I never go to church."

Lucas goes home. All the lights in Grandmother's house are out. The cat and the dog are asleep in the kitchen. The other half of the roast duck stands uneaten on the table.

Lucas tries to go into the bedroom. The door is locked. He knocks. Yasmine doesn't answer.

Lucas goes into town. Candles burn in the windows. The bars are closed. Lucas wanders through the streets for a long time, then he goes into the church. The big church is cold, almost empty. Lucas leans against the wall next to the door. Far off, at the other end of the church, the priest conducts mass at the altar.

Lucas feels a hand on his shoulder. Peter says, "Come on, Lucas. Let's go."

Outside he asks, "What were you doing there?"

"What about you, Peter?"

"I followed you. I saw you as I was leaving Victor's."

Lucas says, "I feel lost in this town when the bars are closed."

"I feel lost here all the time. Come back to my place to warm yourself up before you go home."

Peter lives in a beautiful house in the main square. There are deep armchairs, bookcases covering the walls; it is warm. Peter brings out the brandy.

"I have no friends in this town apart from Victor, who is kind and cultured, but rather boring. He never stops complaining."

Lucas goes to sleep. At daybreak, when he wakes up, Peter is still there, sitting opposite, watching him.

The following summer the child stands upright. Clinging to the dog's back, he shouts, "Lucas! Look! Look!"

Lucas rushes in. The child says, "Mathi is bigger than the dog. Mathi can stand."

The dog moves away, the child falls. Lucas takes him in his arms, he lifts him over his head, he says, "Mathias is bigger than Lucas!"

The child laughs. The next day, Lucas buys him a tricycle.

Yasmine says to Lucas, "You spend too much money on toys."

Lucas says, "The tricycle will help his legs develop."

By autumn the child is walking with confidence, but with a pronounced limp.

One morning, Lucas says to Yasmine, "After lunch, bathe the child and dress him in clean clothes. I'm taking him to a doctor."

"To a doctor? Why?"

"Can't you see he's limping?"

Yasmine replies, "It's a miracle he's even walking."

Lucas says, "I want him to walk like everyone else."

Yasmine's eyes fill with tears. "I accept him as he is."

When the child has been washed and dressed, Lucas takes him by the hand.

"We're going for a long walk, Mathias. When you feel tired, I'll carry you."

Yasmine asks, "You're going to walk across town with him, all the way to the hospital?"

"Why not?"

"People will look at you. You could bump into my aunt."

Lucas doesn't answer.

Yasmine continues, "If they want to keep him, you won't let them, will you, Lucas?"

Lucas says, "What a question!"

When he comes back from the hospital, Lucas says simply, "You were right, Yasmine."

He locks himself in his room, listens to records. When the child beats on his door, he doesn't open it.

That evening, after Yasmine has put the child to bed, Lucas comes into Grandmother's room. As on every other evening he sits beside the cradle and tells Mathias a story. When he finishes the story, he says, "Your cradle will soon be too small for you. I'll have to make you a bed."

The child says, "We'll keep the cradle for the dog and the cat."

"Yes, we'll keep the cradle. I'll also build you some shelves for the books you already own and all the ones I'm going to buy you."

The child says, "Tell me another story."

"I have to go to work."

"People don't work at night."

"I work all the time. I have to earn lots of money."

"What's money for?"

"To buy the things we need, the three of us."

"Clothes and shoes?"

"Yes. And toys, books, and records."

"Toys and books, that's good. Go to work."

Lucas says, "And you go to sleep, so you can grow bigger."

The child says, "I'll never grow bigger, you know that. The doctor said so."

"You misunderstood, Mathias. You will grow. Not as quickly as the other children, but you will grow."

The child asks, "Why not as quickly?"

"Because everyone is different. You won't be as big as the others, but you'll be more intelligent. Your size isn't important. Only intelligence matters."

Lucas goes out. But instead of going into town he goes down to the river. He sits on the damp grass and stares into the dark, muddy water.

3

Lucas says to Victor, "These children's books are all the same. The stories in them are stupid. They're not good enough for a child of four."

Victor shrugs his shoulders. "What can I do? It's the same for adults. Look. Novels written to the greater glory of the regime. You'd think there weren't any writers left in our country."

Lucas says, "Yes, I know those novels. They're not worth the paper they're printed on. What has happened to the old books?"

"Banned. Disappeared. Pulled out of circulation. You might find some at the library, if it still exists."

"A library here in this town? I never knew there was one. Where is it?"

"The first street on the left after the castle. I can't tell you the name of the street, it keeps changing all the time. They're constantly renaming all the streets."

Lucas says, "I'll find it."

The street that Victor described is empty of people. Lucas

waits. An old man comes out of a house. Lucas asks him, "Do you know where the library is?"

The old man points to an old, gray, dilapidated building.

"It's there. But not for much longer, I think. It seems like they're moving out. Every week a truck arrives to take away a load of books."

Lucas goes into the gray building. He goes down a long, dark corridor, which ends at a glass-paneled door with a rusted plaque reading PUBLIC LIBRARY.

Lucas knocks. A woman's voice replies, "Come in!"

Lucas enters a huge room lit by the setting sun. A gray-haired woman is sitting behind a desk. She asks, "What do you want?"

"I'd like to borrow some books."

The woman takes off her glasses and looks at Lucas.

"Borrow some books? Since I've been here no one has come to borrow books."

"Have you been here long?"

"For two years. It's my job to put this place in order. I have to sort out the books and eliminate any that are on the index."

"What happens then? What do you do with them?"

"I put them in boxes and they are taken off to be pulped."

"Are there many books on the index?"

"Almost all of them."

Lucas looks at the large boxes filled with books.

"It's a sad job you've got."

She asks, "Do you like books?"

"I've read all the priest's books. He has a lot, but some of them aren't very interesting."

She smiles. "I can believe that."

"I've also read the ones you can buy in the shops. They are even less interesting."

She smiles again. "What sort of books would you like to read?"

"The books on the index."

She puts her glasses back on. She says, "I'm sorry, that's impossible. Go away now."

Lucas doesn't move. She repeats, "I told you to go away."

Lucas says, "You look like my mother."

"In her younger days, I trust."

"No. My mother was younger than you when she died."

She says, "Forgive me. I'm sorry."

"My mother still had dark hair. You have gray hair and you wear glasses."

The woman gets up. "It's five o'clock. I'm closing."

Out in the street Lucas says, "I'll walk with you. Let me carry your basket. It looks very heavy."

They walk in silence. Near the station, at a small, low house, she stops.

"I live here. Thank you. What is your name?"

"Lucas."

"Thank you, Lucas."

She takes back her basket. Lucas asks, "What's inside it?"

"Charcoal briquettes."

The next day, late in the afternoon, Lucas returns to the library. The gray-haired woman is sitting at her desk.

Lucas says, "You forgot to lend me a book yesterday."

"I told you it's impossible."

Lucas takes a book from one of the big boxes.

"Let me take just one. This one."

She raises her voice. "You haven't even looked at the title. Put that book back in the box and leave!"

Lucas puts the book back in the box.

"Don't get angry. I won't take a book. I'll wait till you close."

"You'll do no such thing! Get out of here, you damn trouble-maker! It's disgraceful, at your age!" She starts sobbing. "When will they stop spying on me, watching me, suspecting me?"

Lucas leaves the library. He sits on the steps of the house opposite. He waits. Shortly after five o'clock the woman comes out, smiling.

"Forgive me. I'm so afraid. Afraid all the time. Of everyone."

Lucas says, "I won't ask you for any more books. I came back only because you remind me of my mother." He takes a photo from his pocket. "Look."

She looks at the photo. "I can't see any resemblance. Your mother is young, beautiful, elegant."

Lucas asks, "Why do you wear flat-heeled shoes, and that colorless dress? Why do you go around like an old woman?"

She says, "I'm thirty-five years old."

"My mother was that old in the photo. You could at least dye your hair."

"My hair went white in the space of a single night. It was the night *they* hanged my husband for high treason. That was three years ago."

She hands her basket to Lucas.

"Walk with me."

Outside her house, Lucas asks, "Can I come in?"

"No one comes into my house."

"Why?"

"I don't know anyone in this town."

"You know me now."

She smiles. "Yes. Come in, Lucas."

In the kitchen, Lucas says, "I don't know your name. I don't want to call you 'madame.' "

"My name is Clara. You can carry the basket into the bedroom and empty it next to the stove. I'll make some tea."

Lucas empties the charcoal briquettes into a wooden box. He goes to the window; he sees the small, overgrown garden, and beyond that a railway embankment infested with weeds.

Clara comes into the room.

"I forgot to buy sugar."

She puts a tray on the table. She comes up to Lucas.

"It's quiet here. There are no trains anymore."

Lucas says, "It's a nice house."

"It's a civil service house. It used to belong to some people who fled the country."

"The furniture too?"

"The furniture in this room, yes. The furniture in the other room is mine. My bed, my desk, my bookcase."

Lucas asks, "Can I see your room?"

"Another time, perhaps. Come and drink your tea."

Lucas takes a sip of bitter tea, then says, "I have to go, I've got work to do. But I could come back later."

She says, "No, don't come back. I go to bed very early to save on charcoal."

When Lucas gets home, Yasmine and Mathias are in the kitchen. Yasmine says, "The little one wouldn't go to bed without you. I've already fed the animals, and I've milked the goats."

Lucas tells Mathias a story. Then he goes to the priest's house. Finally he goes back to the little house on Station Street. There are no lights on.

Lucas waits in the street. Clara comes out of the library. She hasn't got her basket. She says to Lucas, "Surely you don't intend to wait for me every day?"

"Why not? Does it bother you?"

"Yes. It's stupid and pointless."

Lucas says, "I'd like to walk back with you."

"I haven't got my basket. Besides, I'm not going straight home. I've got some shopping to do."

Lucas asks, "Can I come around later this evening?"

"No!"

"Why not? It's Friday today. You don't have to work tomorrow. You don't have to go to bed early."

Clara says, "That's enough! Don't interest yourself in me, or the time I go to bed. Stop waiting for me and following me like a little dog."

"So I won't see you until Monday?"

She sighs and shakes her head. "Not on Monday, not on any day. Stop pestering me, Lucas, please. What do you want from me?"

Lucas says, "I like seeing you. Even in your old dress and with your gray hair."

"Don't be impertinent!"

Clara turns on her heel and heads off in the direction of the main square. Lucas follows her.

Clara goes into a clothes shop, then into a shoe shop. Lucas waits a long time. Then she goes into a grocery shop. She is fully laden as she sets off down the road to Station Street. Lucas catches up with her.

"Let me help you."

Clara speaks without stopping. "Don't bother me! Go away! Don't let me see you again!"

"Very well, Clara. You won't see me again."

Lucas goes home. Yasmine says to him, "Mathias is already in bed."

"Already? Why?"

"I think he's sulking."

Lucas goes into Grandmother's room.

"Are you asleep, Mathias?"

The child doesn't answer. Lucas leaves the room. Yasmine asks, "Will you be back late this evening?"

"It's Friday."

She says, "We make enough from the garden and the animals. You should stop playing in the bars, Lucas. It's not worth spending the whole night there for the few pennies you earn."

Lucas doesn't answer. He does his evening chores and goes to the priest's house.

The priest says, "We haven't played chess for ages."

Lucas says, "I'm very busy at the moment."

He goes into town, enters a bar, plays the harmonica. He drinks. He drinks in all the bars in town, and goes back to Clara's house.

At the kitchen window there is a crack of light through the curtains. Lucas walks around the block, then comes back along the railway line. He goes into Clara's garden. On this side the curtains are thinner; Lucas makes out two silhouettes in the room where he was yesterday. A man paces up and down in the room. Clara is leaning on the stove. The man approaches her, withdraws, approaches her again. He is speaking. Lucas hears his voice but can't make out the words.

The two silhouettes join. They stay like that a long time. They separate. The light goes on in the bedroom. The living room is now empty.

When Lucas goes to the other window, the light goes out.

Lucas goes back to the front of the house. Hidden in the shadows, he waits.

Early in the morning a man leaves Clara's house and walks off quickly. Lucas follows him. The man goes into one of the houses in the main square.

Back home, Lucas goes into the kitchen for a drink of water. Yasmine comes out of Grandmother's room.

"I waited for you all night. It's six o'clock in the morning. Where were you?"

"In the street."

"What's wrong, Lucas?"

She reaches out a hand to touch his face. Lucas brushes it away, walks out of the kitchen, and locks himself in his room.

On Saturday evening, Lucas goes from one bar to another. The people are drunk and generous.

Suddenly, through a cloud of smoke, Lucas sees her. She is sitting alone, near the entrance; she is drinking red wine. Lucas sits at her table.

"Clara! What are you doing here?"

"I couldn't sleep. I wanted to be with people."

"These people?"

"Any people. I can't stay in the house alone, always alone."

"You weren't alone yesterday evening."

Clara doesn't reply, she pours some wine, she drinks. Lucas takes the glass from her hands.

"You've had enough!"

She laughs. "No. I've never had enough. I want to drink and go on drinking."

"Not here! Not with them!"

Lucas grips Clara's wrist. She looks at him, she murmurs, "I was looking for you."

"You didn't want to see me."

She doesn't reply; she turns her head away.

The customers are demanding some music.

Lucas throws some coins onto the table. "Come!"

He takes Clara by the arm, he leads her to the exit. Remarks and rude laughter follow them out.

Outside, it is raining. Clara staggers; she trips on her high heels. Lucas virtually has to carry her.

In her room, she falls onto the bed. She shivers. Lucas takes off her shoes and covers her up. He goes into the other room. He lights a fire in the stove that warms up the two rooms. He makes some tea in the kitchen. He brings two cups.

Clara says, "There's some rum in the kitchen cupboard."

Lucas brings the rum. He pours some into the cups.

Clara says, "You're too young to drink."

Lucas says, "I'm twenty. I learned to drink at the age of twelve."

Clara closes her eyes. "I'm almost old enough to be your mother."

Later she says, "Stay here. Don't leave me alone."

Lucas sits at the desk, he looks around the room. Apart from the bed, there is only the big desk and a small shelf of books. He looks at the books. They are of no interest; he is familiar with them.

Clara sleeps. Her arm is hanging out of the bed. Lucas takes hold of the arm. He kisses the back of the hand, then the palm. He licks it, running his tongue up to her elbow. Clara doesn't move.

It is warm now. Lucas pulls back the eiderdown. Clara's body lies before him, white and black. While Lucas was in the kitchen, Clara took off her skirt and sweater. Now Lucas takes off her black stockings, her black suspenders, her black bra. He covers up her white body with the eiderdown. Then he burns her underwear in the stove in the next room. He pulls up an armchair and settles down next to the bed. He notices a book on the ground. He looks at it. It is an old, worn-out book. The flyleaf bears the library stamp. Lucas reads. The hours pass.

Clara begins to moan. Her eyes remain closed, her face is covered with sweat. She tosses her head from side to side on the pillow and mutters incomprehensibly.

Lucas goes into the kitchen, dampens a cloth and lays it on Clara's forehead. Her mutterings turn into screams.

Lucas shakes her to wake her up. She opens her eyes.

"In the desk drawer. Tranquilizers. A white box."

Lucas finds the tranquilizers. Clara takes two with the remains of the cold tea. She says, "It's nothing. It's always the same nightmare."

She closes her eyes. When her breathing becomes regular, Lucas leaves. He takes the book.

He walks slowly in the rain through the deserted streets to Grandmother's house, on the other side of town.

On Sunday afternoon, Lucas goes back to Clara's house. He knocks on the kitchen door.

Clara asks, "Who is it?"

"It's me, Lucas."

Clara opens the door. She looks pale. She is wearing an old red dressing gown.

"What do you want?"

Lucas says, "I was passing by. I just wondered if you were all right."

"Yes, I feel fine."

Her hand, which holds the door, is trembling.

Lucas says, "Forgive me. I was afraid."

"Of what? You don't need to be afraid on my account."

Lucas whispers, "Clara, please, let me in."

Clara shakes her head. "You're very persistent, Lucas. Come in, then, and have some coffee."

They sit in the kitchen, they drink coffee.

Clara asks, "What happened last night?"

"You don't remember?"

"No. I've been receiving treatment since the death of my husband. The medication I'm on sometimes has a disastrous effect on my memory."

"I brought you home from the bar. If you're under medication you should stay off alcohol."

She buries her face in her hands. "You can't imagine what I've been through."

Lucas says, "I know the pain of separation."

"The death of your mother."

"And something else besides. The loss of a brother who was as one with me."

Clara raises her head. She looks at Lucas.

"We too, Thomas and I, we were a single being. *They* killed him. Did they also kill your brother?"

"No. He went away. He went across the border."

"Why didn't you go with him?"

"One of us had to stay behind to look after the animals, the garden, Grandmother's house. We also had to learn to live without each other. Alone."

Clara rests her hand on Lucas's.

"What is his name?"

"Claus."

"He'll come back. Thomas will never come back."

Lucas gets up. "Do you want me to light the fire in the room? Your hands are frozen."

Clara says, "That would be nice. I'll make some pancakes. I haven't eaten anything today."

Lucas cleans the stove. There is no trace of the black underwear. He lights the fire and comes back into the kitchen.

"There's no charcoal left."

Clara says, "I'll go and get some from the cellar." She picks up a tin bucket.

Lucas says, "Let me do it."

"No! There's no light. I know my way."

Lucas sits in the armchair in the living room. He takes Clara's book out of his pocket. He reads.

Clara brings in the pancakes.

Lucas asks, "Who is he, your lover?"

"You spied on me?"

Lucas says, "It was for him that you bought the black underwear, it was for him that you wore high heels. You should have dyed your hair while you were at it."

Clara says, "That's none of your business. What are you reading?"

Lucas hands her the book.

"I borrowed it from you yesterday. I liked it very much."

"You had no right to take it away with you. I have to return it to the library."

"Don't be angry, Clara. I'm sorry."

Clara turns away.

"What about my underwear? Did you borrow that, too?"

"No. I burned it."

"You burned it? What gave you the right?"

Lucas gets up.

"I think it's best if I leave."

"Yes, go on. They're expecting you."

"Who's expecting me?"

"A wife and child, by all accounts."

"Yasmine is not my wife."

"She's been living with you for four years with her child."

"He's not my child, but he belongs to me now."

On Monday, Lucas waits opposite the library. Evening comes and Clara does not appear. Lucas goes into the old, gray building, walks down the long corridor, knocks at the glass-paneled door. There is no answer; the door is locked.

Lucas runs to Clara's house. He enters without knocking, goes into the kitchen, then the living room. The door to the bedroom is half open. Lucas calls, "Clara?"

"Come in, Lucas."

Lucas goes into the room. Clara is in bed. Lucas sits on the edge of the bed, takes Clara's hand. It is burning hot. He touches her forehead.

"I'll go get a doctor."

"No, it's not worth it. It's only a chill. I've got a headache and a sore throat, that's all."

"Do you have any medicine for aches and fever?"

"No, nothing. I'll see how I feel tomorrow. For now just light the fire and make some tea."

While drinking the tea she says, "Thank you for coming, Lucas."

"You knew I'd come back."

"I hoped so. It's awful being ill when you're on your own."

Lucas says, "You'll never be alone again, Clara."

Clara presses Lucas's hand against her cheek. "I've treated you badly."

"You treated me like a dog. It doesn't matter."

He strokes Clara's hair, which is wet with perspiration.

"Try to sleep. I'll go get some medicine and come back."

"The pharmacy is probably already closed."

"I'll make them open up."

Lucas runs to the main square. He rings the bell of the only pharmacist in town. He rings several times. Finally a small window opens in the wooden door. The pharmacist asks, "What do you want?"

"Medicine for fever and aches. It's urgent."

"Do you have a prescription?"

"I haven't had the time to see a doctor."

"That doesn't surprise me. The problem is that it's more expensive without a prescription."

"That doesn't matter."

Lucas takes a bill from his pocket. The pharmacist brings him a bottle of tablets.

Lucas runs to Grandmother's house. Yasmine and the child are in the kitchen. Yasmine says, "I've already taken care of the animals."

"Thank you, Yasmine. Could you take the priest his meal tonight? I'm in a hurry."

Yasmine says, "I don't know the priest. I don't want to see him."

"You only have to leave the basket on the kitchen table."

Yasmine is silent; she looks at Lucas.

Lucas turns to Mathias. "This evening Yasmine will tell you a story."

The child says, "Yasmine can't tell stories."

"Well, you tell her one. And you can draw me a nice picture."

"Yes, a nice picture."

Lucas goes back to Clara. He dissolves two tablets in a glass of water, he takes it to Clara.

"Drink it."

Clara obeys. Soon she is asleep.

Lucas goes down into the cellar with his flashlight. In the corner there is a small pile of charcoal, and there are sacks lined along the wall. Some of the sacks are open; others are tied up with string. Lucas looks in one of the sacks: it is full of potatoes. He unties the string on another sack: it contains charcoal briquettes. He tips the contents of the sack onto the floor; four or five briquettes and two dozen books fall out. Lucas picks out a book and puts the others back in the sack. He goes back upstairs with the book and the bucket of charcoal.

Sitting beside Clara's bed, he reads.

The next morning, Clara asks, "You stayed here all night?"

"Yes. I slept very well."

He makes some tea, gives Clara the tablets, relights the fire. Clara takes her temperature. She is still feverish.

Lucas says, "Stay in bed. I'll come back at noon. What would you like to eat?"

She says, "I'm not hungry. But can I ask you to go to the council office to tell them I'm out sick?"

"I will. Don't worry."

Lucas goes to the council office. Then he goes home, kills a chicken, and boils it up with some vegetables. At noon, he takes some soup to Clara. She drinks a little.

Lucas says to her, "I went down into the cellar yesterday for the charcoal. I saw the books. You carried them in your basket, didn't you?"

She says, "Yes. I couldn't bear the thought of *them* destroying them all."

"Will you allow me to read them?"

"Read all you want. But be careful. I'm risking imprisonment."

"I know."

In the late afternoon, Lucas goes home. There's nothing to do in the garden at this time of year. Lucas sees to the animals, then listens to records in his room. The child knocks; Lucas lets him in.

The child climbs onto the double bed. He asks, "Why is Yasmine crying?"

"She's crying?"

"Yes. Nearly all the time. Why?"

"Hasn't she told you why?"

"I'm afraid to ask her."

Lucas turns away to change the record.

"She's probably crying for her father, who is in prison."

"What's prison?"

"It's a big building with bars in the windows. They lock people up there."

"Why?"

"For all sorts of reasons. They say that they are dangerous. My father was also locked up."

The child raises his large, dark eyes to Lucas.

"Could they lock you up as well?"

"Yes, me as well."

The child sniffs, his little lip trembles.

"And me?"

Lucas lifts him onto his knees, he kisses him.

"No, not you. They don't lock up children."

"But when I grow up?"

Lucas says, "Things will have changed by then and no one will be locked up anymore."

The child is silent for a moment, then asks, "The ones who are locked up will never be able to get out of prison!"

Lucas says, "They will get out someday."

"Yasmine's father as well?"

"Yes, of course."

"And she'll stop crying?"

"Yes, she'll stop crying."

"And will your father get out too?"

"He already got out."

"Where is he?"

"He's dead. He had an accident."

"If he hadn't got out, he wouldn't have had an accident."

Lucas says, "I have to go now. Go back to the kitchen, and don't talk to Yasmine about her father. You'll make her cry even more. Be nice and obedient to her."

Standing in the kitchen doorway, Yasmine asks, "You're going out, Lucas?"

Lucas halts at the garden gate. He doesn't answer.

Yasmine says, "I'd just like to know if I have to go to the priest's house myself again."

"If you would, Yasmine. I haven't got the time."

Lucas spends his nights by Clara's side until Friday.

On Friday morning Clara says, "I feel better. I'll go back to work on Monday. You don't have to spend your nights here. You've given me so much of your time."

"What do you mean, Clara?"

"I'd like to be alone this evening."

"*He* is coming! Is that it?"

She lowers her eyes and doesn't reply.

Lucas says, "You can't do this to me!"

Clara looks Lucas in the eyes. "You reproached me for acting like an old woman. You were right. I'm still young."

Lucas asks, "Who is he? Why does he only come on Fridays? Why doesn't he marry you?"

"He's already married."

Clara cries.

Lucas asks, "Why are you crying? I should be the one who's crying."

In the evening, Lucas goes to the bar. After closing time, he walks around the streets. It is snowing. Lucas stops in front of Peter's house. The windows are dark. Lucas rings; no one answers. Lucas rings again.

A window opens. Peter asks, "Who's there?"

"It's me. Lucas."

"Stay there, Lucas. I'm coming."

The window closes and soon the door opens. Peter says, "Come in, lost soul."

Peter is in his dressing gown. Lucas says, "I woke you. I'm sorry."

"It's not important. Sit down."

Lucas sits in a leather armchair.

"I can't face going home in this cold. It's too far, and I've had too much to drink. Can I sleep here?"

"Of course, Lucas. Take my bed. I'll sleep on the sofa."

"I prefer the sofa. So I can leave when I wake up without disturbing you."

"As you wish, Lucas. Make yourself comfortable. I'll fetch a blanket."

Lucas takes off his jacket and his boots. He lies down on the sofa. Peter returns with a thick blanket. He lays it over Lucas and puts some cushions under his head. He sits down next to him on the sofa.

"What's wrong, Lucas? Is it about Yasmine?"

Lucas shakes his head. "Everything at home is fine. I just wanted to see you."

Peter says, "I don't believe you."

Lucas takes Peter's hand and presses it to his abdomen. Peter pulls his hand away. He gets up.

"No, Lucas. Don't come into this world of mine."

He goes to his room, closes the door.

Lucas waits. A few hours later he gets up. He opens the door quietly, approaches Peter's bed. Peter is asleep. Lucas leaves the room, closes the door, pulls on his boots, picks up his jacket, checks to see that his weapons are still in the pocket, and leaves the house without a sound. He goes to Station Road. He waits outside Clara's house.

A man leaves the house. Lucas follows him, then passes him on the other side of the street. To get home, the man has to go past a small park. There Lucas hides himself behind some bushes. He wraps the large red scarf knitted by Yasmine around his head, and when the man arrives, he stands up in front of him. He recognizes him. It is one of the doctors from the hospital who examined Mathias.

The doctor says, "Who are you? What do you want?"

Lucas grabs the man by the lapel of his coat, pulls a razor from his pocket.

"If you go to see her again I'll cut your throat."

"You're insane! I've just been on night duty at the hospital."

"Don't bother lying. I'm not joking. I'm capable of anything. Today is just a warning."

Lucas takes a stocking full of gravel from his jacket pocket and strikes the man on the head with it. The man falls senseless to the icy ground.

Lucas goes back to Peter's, lies down on the sofa, and goes to sleep. Peter wakes him at seven o'clock with some coffee.

"I came to check on you earlier. I thought you had gone home."

Lucas says, "I haven't moved from here all night. It's important, Peter."

Peter looks at him long and hard. "I understand, Lucas."

Lucas goes home. Yasmine says to him, "A policeman came. You have to go to the police station. What has happened, Lucas?"

Mathias says, "They are going to lock Lucas up in prison. And Lucas will never come home."

The child snickers. Yasmine grabs his arm and slaps him. "Will you shut up?"

Lucas grabs the child from Yasmine and takes him in his arms. He wipes the tears from his face.

"Don't be afraid, Mathias. They won't lock me up."

The child stares Lucas straight in the eyes. He stops crying. He says, "Too bad."

Lucas presents himself at the police station. He is shown the way to the commissioner's office. Lucas knocks and enters. Clara and the doctor are sitting with a policeman.

The commissioner says, "Hello, Lucas. Sit down."

Lucas sits on a chair next to the man he knocked out a few hours previously.

The commissioner asks, "Do you recognize your attacker, doctor?"

"I wasn't attacked, I told you. I slipped on the ice."

"And you fell on your back. Our officers found you lying on your back. It's strange that you have a lump on your forehead."

"I probably fell forward, then turned over as I began to regain consciousness."

The commissioner says, "Of course. You claim that you were on night duty at the hospital. According to our information you left the hospital at nine o'clock in the evening, and you spent the night with this lady."

The doctor says, "I didn't want to compromise her."

The commissioner turns to Lucas. "The lady's neighbors have seen you enter her house on numerous occasions."

Lucas says, "I've been doing her shopping for her for some time. Especially last week when she was ill."

"We know that you didn't go home last night. Where were you?"

"I was too tired to go home. When the bars closed I went to a friend's house and spent the night there. I left at half past seven."

"Who is this friend? A drinking buddy, I suppose."

"No. He's the Party Secretary."

"You claim you spent the night at the Party Secretary's house?"

"Yes. He made me some coffee at seven o'clock this morning."

The commissioner leaves the room.

The doctor turns to Lucas, stares at him. Lucas returns his gaze. The doctor looks at Clara. Clara looks out of the window.

The doctor stares straight ahead; he says, "I haven't brought charges against you, even though I recognize you perfectly. It was some border guards on patrol who found me and brought me here, like a common drunk. This is all very unfortunate for me. I ask you for your total discretion. I am an internationally renowned psychiatrist. I have children."

Lucas says, "Your only solution is to leave this town. It's a small town. Sooner or later, everyone will know. Even your wife."

"Is that a threat?"

"Yes."

"I've been assigned to this godforsaken hole. It's not for me to decide where I go."

"It doesn't matter. Ask for a transfer."

The commissioner comes in with Peter. Peter looks at Lucas, then at Clara, then at the doctor. The commissioner says, "Your alibi is confirmed, Lucas."

He turns to the doctor. "I think we'll leave it there, doctor. You slipped while returning from the hospital. The case is closed."

The doctor asks Peter, "Can I see you on Monday at your office? I wish to leave this town."

Peter says, "Certainly. You can count on my help."

The doctor gets up, offers Clara his hand. "I'm sorry."

Clara turns her head away. The doctor leaves the room, saying, "Thank you, gentlemen."

Lucas says to Clara, "I'll walk you home."

Clara goes out ahead of him without saying a word.

Lucas and Peter also leave the commissioner's office. Peter watches Clara leave. "So it was because of her."

Lucas says, "Do everything you can, Peter, to get this man transferred. If he stays in this town he's a dead man."

Peter says, "I believe you. You're crazy enough to do it. Don't worry. He'll leave. But if she loved him, do you realize what you've done to her?"

Lucas says, "She doesn't love him."

It is already almost noon when Lucas gets home from the police station.

The child says, "They didn't lock you up?"

Yasmine says, "I hope it was nothing serious."

Lucas says, "No. Everything is all right. They needed me as a witness to a fight."

Yasmine says, "You'd better go and see the priest. He's stopped eating. He hasn't touched anything I took him yesterday or the day before."

Lucas takes a bottle of goat's milk and goes to the priest's house. The congealed food stands on the kitchen table. The stove is cold. Lucas crosses an empty room and enters the bedroom without knocking. The priest is in bed.

Lucas asks, "Are you ill?"

"No, I'm just cold. I'm always cold."

"I brought you enough wood. Why don't you warm yourself up?"

The priest says, "I have to economize. On wood and everything else."

"You're just too lazy to light the fire."

"I am old, I don't have enough strength left."

"You don't have enough strength because you don't eat."

"I have no appetite. Since you no longer bring the meals, I have no appetite."

Lucas hands him his dressing gown. "Get dressed and come to the kitchen."

He helps the old man into his dressing gown, he helps him to walk to the kitchen, he helps him to sit on the bench. He pours him a cup of milk. The priest drinks.

Lucas says, "You can't go on living on your own. You are too old."

The priest puts his cup down. He looks at Lucas.

"I'm leaving, Lucas. My superiors have recalled me. I'm going to retire to a monastery. There won't be a priest in this town anymore. The priest from the neighboring town will come once a week to celebrate mass."

"It's a sensible decision. I'm happy for you."

"I will miss this town. I've been here for forty-five years."

After a silence, the priest continues. "You have taken care of me all these years as if you were my own son. I would like to thank you. But how can I repay you for so much love and so much goodness?"

"Don't thank me. There is no love and no goodness in me."

"That's what you think, Lucas. I'm convinced of the contrary. You have suffered a wound from which you have not yet recovered."

Lucas is silent. The priest continues. "I feel that I am leaving you during a particularly difficult time in your life, but I will be with you in spirit and I will pray always for the salvation of your soul. You have taken the wrong course. I sometimes wonder where you will end up. Your passionate and tortured nature can drive you to the worst extremes. But I live in hope. God's mercy is infinite."

The priest gets up and takes Lucas's face in his hands. " 'Remember now thy Creator in the days of thy youth, while the evil days come not, nor the years draw nigh, when thou shalt say, I have no pleasure in them. . . .' "

Lucas lowers his head; his forehead rests on the priest's chest.

" 'While the sun, or the light, or the moon, or the stars, be not darkened, nor the clouds return after the rain. . . .' It's Ecclesiastes."

The priest's frail body shakes with sobbing. "Yes. You recognized it. You still remember. When you were a child you knew entire pages of the Bible by heart. Do you still find the time to read it sometimes?"

Lucas frees himself. "I've got a lot of work. And I have other books to read."

The priest says, "I understand. I also know that my sermons bore you. Go now, and don't come back. I'm leaving tomorrow on the first train."

Lucas says, "I wish you a peaceful retirement, Father."

He goes home. He says to Yasmine, "The priest is going away tomorrow. There's no need to take him food anymore."

The child asks, "Is he leaving because you don't love him anymore? Yasmine and me, we'll leave too if you don't love us anymore."

Yasmine says, "Be quiet, Mathias!"

The child cries out, "She's the one who said it! But you do love us, don't you, Lucas?"

Lucas takes him in his arms. "Of course, Mathias."

At Clara's house the fire is burning in the living-room stove. The bedroom door is open.

Lucas goes into the room. Clara is in bed, with a book in her hands. She looks at Lucas, shuts the book, puts it on the bedside table.

Lucas says, "I'm sorry, Clara."

Clara throws back the quilt covering her. She is naked. She continues staring at Lucas.

"It's what you wanted, isn't it?"

"I don't know. I really don't know, Clara."

Clara switches off the bedside lamp. "What are you waiting for?"

Lucas lights the desk lamp, points it at the bed. Clara closes her eyes.

Lucas kneels by the bed, opens Clara's legs, then the lips of her vulva. A thin trickle of blood comes out. He bends forward; he licks and drinks the blood. Clara moans; her hands grasp Lucas's hair.

Lucas gets undressed, lies on top of Clara, enters her, cries out. Later, Lucas gets up, opens the window. Outside it is snowing. Lucas returns to the bed. Clara takes him in her arms. Lucas shivers. She says, "Calm yourself."

She strokes Lucas's hair, his face. He asks, "You're not angry with me about him?"

"No. It's better that he left."

Lucas says, "I knew you didn't love him. You were so unhappy last week when I saw you in the bar."

Clara says, "I met him at the hospital. It was he who took care of me when I had another depression during the summer. The fourth since Thomas died."

"Do you often dream of Thomas?"

"Every night. But only of his execution. Never of Thomas happy, alive."

Lucas says, "I see my brother everywhere. In my room, in the garden, walking beside me in the street. He speaks to me."

"What does he say?"

"He says he is living in mortal solitude."

Lucas goes to sleep in Clara's arms. In the middle of the night he enters her again, softly, slowly, as if in a dream.

From then on, Lucas spends all his nights at Clara's.

The winter is very cold this year. The sun doesn't appear for five months. An icy mist lies stagnant on the deserted town. The ground is frozen, the river too.

In the kitchen of Grandmother's house, the fire is on all the time. The firewood runs out quickly. Every afternoon, Lucas goes into the forest to find wood, which he sets to dry next to the stove.

The kitchen door is left open to warm the room of Yasmine and her child. Lucas's room is not heated.

When Yasmine sews or knits in the room, Lucas sits with the child on the large rug made by Yasmine that covers the kitchen floor, and they play together with the dog and the cat. They look at picture books; they draw. Lucas teaches Mathias to count on an abacus.

Yasmine prepares the evening meal. They all sit on the corner seat in the kitchen. They eat potatoes, dried beans, or cabbage. The child doesn't like this food and eats little. Lucas makes him jam tarts.

After the meal, Yasmine washes up. Lucas carries the child into the bedroom, undresses him, puts him to bed and tells him a story. When the child falls asleep, Lucas goes off to Clara's house on the other side of town.

4

On Station Road the chestnut trees are in bloom. Their white petals lie so deep on the ground that Lucas can't even hear the sound of his footsteps. He is coming back from Clara's house, late at night.

The child is sitting on the corner seat in the kitchen. Lucas says, "It's only five o'clock. Why are you up so early?"

The child asks, "Where is Yasmine?"

"She's gone to the big city. She was bored here."

The child's dark eyes open wide. "Gone? Without me?"

Lucas turns away, he lights the fire in the stove.

The child asks, "Is she coming back?"

"No, I don't think so."

Lucas pours some goat's milk into a pan, which he sets to boil.

The child asks, "Why didn't she take me with her? She promised to take me with her."

Lucas says, "She thought you'd be better off here with me, and I agreed."

The child says, "I'm not better off here with you. I'd be better off anywhere else with her."

Lucas says, "A big city is no fun for a child. There are no gardens or animals."

The child says, "But my mother's there."

He looks out of the window. When he turns around his little face is contorted with sorrow.

"She doesn't love me because I'm crippled. That's why she left me here."

"That's not true, Mathias. She loves you with all her heart. You know that."

"Then she will come back to get me."

The child pushes away his cup, his plate, and leaves the kitchen. Lucas goes to water the garden. The sun is rising.

The dog is asleep beneath a tree. The child approaches him with a stick. Lucas watches the child. The child lifts the stick and hits the dog. The dog runs off howling. The child looks at Lucas.

"I don't like animals. I don't like gardens either."

With his stick the child starts thrashing the greens, the tomatoes, the pumpkins, the beans, the flowers. Lucas watches him without saying a word.

The child goes back to the house, he gets into Yasmine's bed. Lucas follows him, he sits on the edge of the bed.

"Are you so unhappy about staying with me? Why?"

The child stares at the ceiling. "Because I hate you."

"You hate me?"

"Yes, I've always hated you."

"I didn't know. Can you tell me why?"

"Because you're big and handsome, and because I thought Yasmine loved you. But if she's gone, it's because she didn't love you either. I hope you're as unhappy as I am."

Lucas puts his head in his hands.

The child asks, "Are you crying?"

"No, I'm not crying."

"But you're sad because of Yasmine?"

"No, not because of Yasmine. I'm sad because of you, because you're sad."

"Is that right? Because of me? That's nice." He smiles. "However, I'm just a little cripple, and she's beautiful."

After a silence the child asks, "Where is your mother?"

"She's dead."

"Was she too old? Is that why she died?"

"No. She died because of the war. She was killed by a shell, together with her baby, who was my little sister."

"Where are they now?"

"The dead are nowhere and everywhere."

The child says, "They're in the attic. I've seen them. The big bone thing and the little bone thing."

Lucas asks in a low voice, "You went up into the attic? How did you get up there?"

"I climbed. It's easy. I'll show you."

Lucas is silent. The child says, "Don't be afraid, I won't tell anyone. I don't want them to take them away. I like them."

"You like them?"

"Yes. Especially the baby. It's smaller and uglier than me. And it will never grow. I didn't know it was a girl. You can't tell when it's just those bone things."

"Those things are called skeletons."

"Yes. Skeletons. I've also seen some in the big book on top of your bookcase."

Lucas and the child are in the garden. A rope hangs from the attic, just within the reach of Lucas's outstretched arm. He says to the child, "Show me how you climb up."

The child pulls the nearby garden bench under the window of Lucas's room. He climbs onto the bench, jumps and grabs the rope, stops it swinging by pressing his feet against the wall, and uses his arms and legs to hoist himself up to the attic door. Lucas follows him. They sit on a mattress, looking at the skeletons hanging from a beam.

The child asks, "Didn't you keep your brother's skeleton?"

"Who told you I had a brother?"

"No one. I've heard you talking to him. You talk to him, and he's nowhere and everywhere, so he must be dead as well."

Lucas says, "No, he's not dead. He's gone to another country. He will return."

"Like Yasmine. She'll return too."

"Yes, both my brother and your mother."

The child says, "That's the only difference between the dead and those who go away, isn't it? Those who aren't dead will return."

Lucas says, "But how do we know they aren't dead when they're away?"

"We can't know."

The child is silent for a moment, then asks, "What did you feel when your brother went away?"

"I didn't know how to go on living without him."

"And do you know now?"

"Yes. Since you came here, I know."

The child opens the chest.

"What are these notebooks in the chest?"

Lucas closes the chest.

"It's nothing. Thank God you can't read yet!"

The child laughs. "Oh yes I can. I can read if it's printed. Look."

He opens the chest and takes out Grandmother's old Bible. He reads words, entire phrases.

Lucas asks, "Where did you learn to read?"

"From books, of course. From mine and yours."

"With Yasmine?"

"No, on my own. Yasmine doesn't like reading. She said she'd never send me to school. But I'll be going soon, won't I, Lucas?"

Lucas says, "I could teach you everything you need to know."

The child says, "School is compulsory from the age of six."

"Not for you. You can get a dispensation."

"Because I'm a cripple, you mean? I don't want your dispensation. I want to go to school like the other children."

Lucas says, "If you want to go, you can. But why do you want to?"

"Because I know I'll be the best at school, the most intelligent."

Lucas laughs. "And the most vain, no doubt. I always hated school. I pretended to be deaf so I wouldn't have to go."

"You did that?"

"Yes. Listen, Mathias. You may come up here whenever you want. You may also go into my room, even when I'm not there. You may read the Bible, the dictionary, the entire encyclopedia if you wish. But you must never read the notebooks, you son of a bitch."

He adds, "Grandmother called us that: sons of a bitch."

"Who's 'us'? You and who else? You and your brother?"

"Yes. My brother and me."

They climb down from the attic, they go into the kitchen. Lucas prepares the meal. The child asks, "Who'll do the dishes, the washing, the clothes?"

"We will. Together. You and I."

They eat. Lucas leans out the window, he throws up. He turns around, his face bathed in sweat. He loses consciousness and falls to the floor of the kitchen.

The child cries, "Don't do that, Lucas, don't do that!"

Lucas opens his eyes. "Don't cry, Mathias. Help me to get up."

The child pulls him by the arm. Lucas clings to the table. He staggers out of the kitchen, he sits on the garden bench. The child stands before him, looking at him.

"What's wrong, Lucas? You were dead for a moment!"

"No, I just felt faint because of the heat."

The child asks, "It doesn't matter that she left, does it? It's not so serious, is it? You won't die because of that?"

Lucas doesn't answer. The child sits at his feet, hugs his legs, lays his head with its dark, curly hair on Lucas's knees.

"Maybe I'll be your son later."

When the child goes to sleep, Lucas goes back into the attic. He takes the notebooks from the chest, wraps them in a jute cloth, and goes into town.

He rings at Peter's.

"I'd like you to keep these for me, Peter."

He puts the packet on the living-room table.

Peter asks, "What is it?"

Lucas pulls open the cloth. "Some school notebooks."

Peter shakes his head. "It's like Victor said. You write. You buy huge quantities of paper and pencils. For years now, pencils, lined paper, and large school notebooks. Are you writing a book?"

"No, not a book. I simply make notes."

Peter feels the weight of the notebooks. "Notes! Half a dozen thick notebooks."

"It accumulates over the years. Even so, I reject a lot. I only keep what's absolutely necessary."

Peter asks, "Why do you want to hide them? Because of the police?"

"The police? Of course not! It's because of the child. He's beginning to learn to read and he gets into everything. I don't want him to read these notebooks."

Peter smiles. "And you don't want the child's mother to read them either, do you?"

Lucas says, "Yasmine is no longer living with me. She's gone away. She has always dreamed of going to the big city. I gave her some money."

"And she left her child with you?"

"I insisted on keeping him."

Peter lights a cigarette and looks at Lucas without speaking.

Lucas asks, "Can you keep these notebooks here, yes or no?"

"Of course I can."

Peter wraps up the notebooks, carries them into his bedroom. When he comes back he says, "I've hidden them under my bed. I'll find a better hiding place tomorrow."

Lucas says, "Thank you, Peter."

Peter laughs. "Don't thank me. Your notebooks interest me."

"You intend to read them?"

"Of course. If you don't want me to read them you should take them to Clara."

Lucas gets up. "Certainly not! Clara reads everything there is to read. But I could give them to Victor."

"In which case I would read them at Victor's. He can't refuse me anything. Anyway, he's leaving soon. He's going back to his hometown to live with his sister. He intends to sell his house and the shop."

Lucas says, "Give me the notebooks back. I'll bury them somewhere in the forest."

"Yes, bury them. Or better still, burn them. It's the only way of preventing people from reading them."

Lucas says, "I have to keep them. For Claus. These notebooks are for Claus. For him alone."

Peter turns on the radio. He fiddles with the dial until he finds some soft music.

"Sit down, Lucas, and tell me, who is Claus?"

"My brother."

"I didn't know you had a brother. You've never mentioned him. Nobody has, not even Victor, and he's known you since childhood."

Lucas says, "My brother has been living on the other side of the border for several years."

"How did he get across the border? It's supposed to be impossible."

"He got across, that's all."

After a silence, Peter asks, "Do you keep in touch with him?"

"What do you mean, keep in touch?"

"What everyone means. Do you write to him? Does he write to you?"

"I write to him every day in the notebooks. Undoubtedly he does the same."

"But don't you get any letters from him?"

"He can't send letters from over there."

"Lots of letters arrive from the other side of the border. Your brother hasn't written since he left? He hasn't given you his address?"

Lucas shakes his head. He gets up again.

"You think he's dead, don't you? Well, Claus isn't dead. He's alive and he will return."

"Yes, Lucas. Your brother will return. As for the notebooks, I could have promised not to read them, but you wouldn't have believed me."

"You're right, I wouldn't have believed you. I knew you wouldn't be able to prevent yourself from reading them. I knew when I came here. So read them. I'd rather it were you than Clara or anyone else."

Peter says, "That's something else I don't understand: your relationship with Clara. She's much older than you."

"Age doesn't matter. I'm her lover. Is that all you wanted to know?"

"No, that's not all. I knew that already. But do you love her?"

Lucas opens the door.

"I don't know the meaning of that word. No one does. I didn't expect that sort of question from you, Peter."

"Nevertheless, you will be asked that sort of question many times in the course of your life. And sometimes you will be obliged to answer it."

"And you, Peter? One day you will also be obliged to answer certain questions. I've been to some of your political meetings. You make speeches, the audience applauds. Do you really believe in what you say?"

"I have to believe it."

"But in your deepest self, what do you think?"

"I don't think. I can't allow myself the luxury. I've lived with fear since I was a child."

* * *

Clara is standing in front of the window, looking out into the garden engulfed in darkness. She doesn't turn around when Lucas comes into the room.

She says, "The summer is frightening. It is in the summer that death is closest. Everything dries out, suffocates, comes to a standstill. It's already been four years since they killed Thomas. In August, very early in the morning, at dawn. They hanged him. The disturbing thing is that they start again every year. At dawn, when you go home, I go to the window and I see them. They are starting again, but you can't kill the same person over and over."

Lucas kisses Clara on the neck.

"What's wrong, Clara? What's wrong with you today?"

"Today I received a letter. An official letter. It's there on my desk, you can read it. It exonerates Thomas, proclaims his innocence. I never doubted his innocence. They write: 'Your husband was innocent. We killed him by mistake. We killed many people by mistake, but at present everything is being sorted out. We apologize and promise that such mistakes will not be allowed to happen in the future.' They murder and they exonerate. They apologize, but Thomas is dead! Can they bring him back to life? Can they wipe out that night when my hair went white, when I went mad?

"That summer night I was alone in our apartment, in Thomas's and my apartment. I'd been alone there for several months. Since they had imprisoned Thomas no one wanted to visit me, no one could, no one dared. I was already used to being alone, it wasn't unusual that I was alone. I didn't sleep, but that wasn't unusual either. What was unusual was that I didn't cry that night. The previous evening the radio announced the execution of a number of people for high treason. Among the names I clearly heard Thomas's name. At three o'clock in the morning, the time of the executions, I looked at the clock. I kept looking at it until seven o'clock, then I went to my job in a large library in the capital. I sat at my desk. I was in charge of the reading room. One after the other my colleagues came up. I heard them whisper, 'She's come!' 'Have you seen her hair?' I left the library, I walked around the streets until evening, I got lost, I didn't know which part of town I was in, even though I knew the town well. I came home in a taxi. At three o'clock in the morning I looked out the window, and I saw them: they were hanging Thomas from the front of the building opposite. I screamed. Some neighbors came. An ambulance took me to the hospital. And now they say it was just a mistake. Thomas's murder, my illness, the months in the hospital, my white hair were just a mistake. Well, let them bring me Thomas alive, smiling. The Thomas who took me in his arms, who stroked my hair, who held my face in his warm hands, who kissed me on the eyes, the ears, the mouth."

Lucas takes Clara by the shoulders, he turns her to face him.

"Will you never stop talking to me about Thomas?"

"Never. I'll never stop talking about Thomas. And you? When will you start talking to me about Yasmine?"

Lucas says, "There's nothing to say. Especially since she's no longer here."

Clara punches and scratches Lucas on the face, the neck, the shoulders. She cries, "She's no longer here? Where is she? What have you done with her?"

Lucas drags Clara onto the bed, he lies on top of her.

"Calm down. Yasmine has gone to the big city, that's all."

Clara grips Lucas in her arms.

"They will separate me from you as they separated me from Thomas. They will put you in prison, take you away."

"No, that's all over. Forget Thomas, the prison, and the rope."

At dawn, Lucas gets up.

"I have to go home. The child wakes up early."

"Yasmine left her child here?"

"He's crippled. What would she have done with him in a big city?"

Clara says, "How could she have left him?"

Lucas says, "She wanted to take him. I forbade her."

"Forbade her? By what right? He's her child. He belongs to her."

Clara watches Lucas get dressed. She says, "Yasmine left because you didn't love her."

"I helped her when she was in trouble. I never promised her anything."

"You've never promised me anything either."

Lucas goes home to prepare breakfast for Mathias.

Lucas goes into the bookshop. Victor asks him, "Do you need any paper or pencils, Lucas?"

"No. I'd like to talk to you. Peter said that you wanted to sell your house."

Victor sighs. "These days nobody has enough money to buy a house with a shop."

Lucas says, "I'd like to buy it."

"You, Lucas? With what, my boy?"

"By selling Grandmother's house. The army has offered a good price for it."

"I'm afraid it wouldn't be enough, Lucas."

"I also own a good plot of land. And other things besides. Very valuable things that I inherited from Grandmother."

Victor says, "Come and see me this evening at the apartment. I'll leave the front door open."

That evening, Lucas goes up the narrow, dark stairway that leads to the apartment above the bookshop. He knocks at the door, below which there is a crack of light.

Victor shouts, "Come in, Lucas!"

Lucas enters a room filled with a thick cloud of cigar smoke, in spite of the open window. The ceiling is stained a dirty brown color, the net curtains are yellowed. The room is crammed with old furniture, divans, sofas, small tables, lamps, trinkets. The walls are covered with paintings, etchings, the floor with layers of threadbare rugs.

Victor is sitting next to the window at a table covered with a red plush tablecloth. On the table are boxes of cigars and cigarettes. Ashtrays of all shapes and sizes full of cigarette butts stand next to glasses and a half-empty carafe of yellow liquid.

"Come in, Lucas. Sit down and have a drink."

Lucas sits down; Victor pours him a drink, drinks up his own glass, refills it.

"I wish I could offer you a better brandy than this, some of the stuff my sister brought on her last visit, for example, but I'm afraid there's none left. My sister came in July. It was very warm, if you remember. I don't like the heat, I don't like summer. A cool, wet summer, fine, but these dog days make me feel positively ill.

"When she came my sister brought me a liter of apricot brandy such as we drink at home in the country. My sister probably thought the bottle would last all year, or at least until Christmas. In fact I'd already drunk half the bottle by the first evening. I was ashamed, so I hid the bottle, then I went to buy a bottle of cheap brandy—it's all you can get in the shops—and used it to top off my sister's bottle, which I left out in an obvious place, there on the sideboard in front of you.

"So by drinking the cheap brandy every evening in secret, I was able to fool my sister by showing her the level in her bottle hardly going down at all. Once or twice, for appearance's sake, I would pour a small glass of this brandy, which I pretended to appreciate, even though it was already quite diluted.

"I waited patiently for my sister to go. Not that she was in the way, quite the opposite. She made my meals, she darned my socks, mended my clothes, cleaned the kitchen and everything else that was dirty. So she was useful, and what's more, we would have pleasant chats over a good meal after I closed the shop. She slept in the small room here at the side. She went to bed early and slept soundly. I had the whole night to myself to walk up and down in my room and in the kitchen and the corridor.

"You must realize, Lucas, that my sister is the person I love most in the world. Our father and mother died when we were young, me especially, since I was still a child. My sister was a little older, five years older. We lived with various relatives, uncles and aunts, but I assure you it was really my sister who brought me up.

"My love for her hasn't diminished in all this time. You will never know the joy I felt when I saw her getting off the train. I hadn't seen her for twelve years. There was the war, poverty, the border zone. When she managed to save enough money for the journey, for instance, she couldn't get a permit for the zone, and so on. For my part, I never have very much ready cash, and I can't just close up the bookshop when I want. And she can't simply walk out on her clients. She's a dressmaker, and even when times are hard women need a dressmaker. Especially during the hard times when they can't afford to buy new clothes. My sister had to work miracles during the hard times. Turning their dead husbands' trousers into short skirts, their nightgowns into blouses, and as for the children's clothes, any old bit of material would do.

"When my sister finally managed to get enough money and the necessary papers and permits, she wrote to tell me she was coming."

Victor gets up, looks out the window.

"It must be ten o'clock by now."

Lucas says, "No, not yet."

Victor sits down again, pours a drink, lights a cigar.

"I waited for my sister at the station. It was the first time I had ever waited for someone at that station. I was ready to wait for several trains if necessary. My sister arrived on the very last train. She had been traveling all day. Of course I recognized her immediately, but she was so different from the image I had of her in my memory! She had become really small. She had always been petite, but not that much. Her—I have to admit—grumpy face was now lined with hundreds of tiny wrinkles. In a word, she had really aged. Naturally, I said nothing, I kept these observations to myself. She, on the other hand, started crying and said, 'Oh, Victor! You've changed so much! I hardly recognize you. You've put on weight, you've lost your hair, you've let yourself go.'

"I carried her cases. They were heavy, stuffed with jam, sausages, apricot brandy. She unpacked it all in the kitchen. She had even brought some beans from her garden. I tasted the brandy straight away. While she was cooking the beans I drank about a quarter of the bottle. After washing up she came to join me in my room. The windows were wide open, it was very hot. I kept on drinking. I constantly went over to the window, smoked cigars. My sister talked about her awkward clients, her difficult, solitary life. I listened to her while drinking brandy and smoking cigars.

"The window opposite lit up at ten o'clock. The man with white hair appeared. He was chewing something. He always eats at that hour. At ten o'clock in the evening he sits at his window and eats. My sister was still talking. I showed her her room and said to her, 'You must be tired. You've had a long journey. Go and rest.' She kissed me on both cheeks, went into the small bedroom at the side, got into bed, and slept, I suppose. I kept on drinking, walking up and down smoking cigars. Now and then I looked out the window. I saw the white-haired man leaning out of his window. I heard him ask the infrequent passersby, 'What time is it? Could you tell me the time, please?' Someone in the street answered, 'It's twenty past eleven.'

"I slept very badly. The silent presence of my sister in the other room disturbed me. The next morning, I heard the insomniac asking the time again, and someone replying, 'It's quarter to seven.' Later, when I got up, my sister was already working in the kitchen; the window opposite was closed.

"What do you think of that, Lucas? My sister, whom I haven't seen for twelve years, comes to visit me, and I can't wait for her to go to bed so I can observe the insomniac across the street in peace—the fact is, he's the only person who interests me, even though I love my sister above all.

"You're saying nothing, Lucas, but I know what you're thinking. You think I'm mad, and you're right. I'm obsessed by this old man who opens his window at ten o'clock at night and closes it again at seven o'clock in the morning. He spends the whole night at his window. I don't know what he does after that. Does he sleep, or does he have another room or a kitchen where he spends the day? I never see him in the street, I never see him during the day, I don't know him and I've never asked anyone anything about him. You're the first person I've talked to about him. What does he think about all night, leaning out of his window? How can we know? By midnight the street is completely empty. He can't even ask the time from the passersby. He can't do that until six or seven in the morning. Does he really need to know the time? Is it possible he doesn't own a watch or an alarm clock? In that case how does he manage to appear at his window at precisely ten o'clock in the evening? There are so many questions I ask myself about him.

"One evening, after my sister had already left, the insomniac spoke to me. I was at my window. I was looking out for the storm clouds that had been forecast for days. The old man spoke to me from across the street. He said, 'You can't see the stars. The storm is coming.' I didn't reply. I looked elsewhere, left and right up the street. I didn't want to strike up an acquaintance. I ignored him.

"I sat in a corner of my room where he couldn't see me. I realize now that if I stay here I'll do nothing but drink, smoke, and watch the insomniac through the window, until I become an insomniac myself."

Victor looks out the window and collapses into his armchair with a sigh. "He's there. He's there and he's watching me. He's waiting for a chance to strike up a conversation with me. But I won't let him, he might as well give up, he won't have the last word."

Lucas says, "Calm down, Victor. Maybe he's just a retired night watchman who got used to sleeping during the day."

Victor says, "A night watchman? Perhaps. It makes no difference. If I stay here, he'll destroy me. I'm already half mad. My sister noticed. Before she got on the train she said, 'I'm too old to make such a long and tiring journey again. We should make a decision, Victor, otherwise I'm afraid we might never see each other again.' I asked, 'What kind of decision?' She said, 'Your business is failing, I can see that much. You sit all day in the shop and never get any customers. At night you walk up and down in the apartment and in the morning you're exhausted. You drink too much—you've drunk nearly half the brandy I brought you. If you go on like that you'll become an alcoholic.'

"I didn't tell her that during her stay I had drunk six other bottles of brandy as well as the bottles of wine we opened at each meal. I didn't tell her about the insomniac either, of course. She continued, 'You look terrible, you have rings round your eyes, you're pale and overweight. You eat too much meat, you get no exercise, you never go out, you lead an unhealthy life.' I said, 'Don't worry about me. I feel fine.' I lit a cigar. The train was late. My sister turned her head away in disgust. 'You smoke too much. You never stop smoking.'

"I didn't tell her that two years ago the doctors discovered that I had an arterial disease caused by nicotine poisoning. My right iliac artery is blocked, there is no circulation, or hardly any, in my left leg. I get pains in my hip and my calf, and I have no feeling in the big toe of my left foot. The doctors gave me medicine, but there will be no improvement if I don't stop smoking and don't start getting exercise. But I have no desire to stop smoking. In fact I'm totally lacking in willpower. You can't expect an alcoholic to have willpower. So if I want to stop smoking, I will first of all have to stop drinking.

"I sometimes think that I should give up smoking, and then right away I light up a cigar or a cigarette, and I think while I'm smoking it that if I don't stop smoking it will soon mean the end of all circulation in my left leg, which will bring about gangrene, which in turn will mean amputation of my foot or the whole leg.

"I said nothing about any of this so as not to worry my sister, but she was worried anyway. As she got on the train she said,

'Sell the bookshop and come live with me in the country. We can live on next to nothing, in the house we grew up in. We can go for walks in the forest. I'll take care of everything. You'll stop smoking and drinking and you can write your book.'

"The train left. I went home, I poured myself a glass of brandy, and wondered what book she was talking about.

"That evening I took a sleeping pill, along with my usual medicine for my circulation, and I drank all the brandy left in my sister's bottle, about half a liter. In spite of the sleeping pill I woke up very early the next morning, with a total lack of sensation in my left leg. I was bathed in perspiration, my heart was pounding, my hands were shaking, I was immersed in a foul and fearful anguish. I checked the time on my alarm clock. It had stopped. I dragged myself to the window. The old man opposite was still there. I called across the empty street, 'Could you tell me the time, please? My watch has stopped.' He turned away, as if consulting a clock, before replying, 'It is half past six.' I was going to get dressed but found that I already was. I had slept in my clothes and my shoes. I went down into the street, I went to the nearest grocery. It was still closed. I walked up and down in the street while I waited. The manager arrived, he opened the shop, he served me. I bought the first bottle of brandy I saw, went home. I drank a few glasses, my anguish disappeared, the man across the street had closed his window.

"I went down to the bookshop, I sat down at the counter. There were no customers. It was still summer, the school holidays, no one needed books or anything else. Sitting there, looking at the books on the shelves, I remembered my book, the book my sister mentioned, the book I had been intending to write since I was a young man. I wanted to become a writer, to write books, that was the dream of my youth, and we often talked about it together, my sister and I. She believed in me, I also believed in myself, but less and less until finally I completely forgot this dream of writing books.

"I'm only fifty years old. If I stop smoking and drinking, or rather drinking and smoking, I can still write a book. Not books, but a single book, perhaps. I am convinced, Lucas, that every human being is born to write a book, and for no other reason. A work of genius or mediocrity, it doesn't matter, but he who writes nothing is lost, he has merely passed through life without leaving a trace.

"If I stay here I will never write a book. My only hope is to sell the house and the shop and go live with my sister. She will keep me from drinking and smoking, we will lead a healthy life, she will take care of everything, I will have nothing else to do except write my book, once I'm rid of the alcoholism and the nicotine poisoning. You yourself, Lucas, are writing a book. About whom, about what, I don't know. But you write. Since you were a child you have never stopped buying sheets of paper, pencils, notebooks."

Lucas says, "You're right, Victor. Writing is the most important thing. Name your price. I'll buy the house and the bookshop. We can close the deal in a few weeks."

Victor asks, "The valuables you mentioned—what are they?"

"Gold and silver coins. And jewels as well."

Victor smiles. "Do you want to inspect the house?"

"That's not necessary. I'll make whatever changes are needed. These two rooms will be enough for the two of us."

"There were three of you, if I remember correctly."

"There are only two of us now. The child's mother has gone away."

* * *

Lucas says to the child, "We're moving. We'll be living in town, in the main square. I bought the bookshop."

The child says, "That's good. I'll be closer to school. But when Yasmine comes back, how will she find us?"

"In a town this size she'll find us easily."

The child asks, "Will we not have a garden and animals anymore?"

"We'll have a little garden. We'll keep the dog and the cat, and some chickens for the eggs. We'll sell the other animals to Joseph."

"Where will I sleep? There's no Grandmother's room there."

"You'll sleep in a little room next to mine. We'll be right next to each other."

"Without the animals and the produce from the garden, what will we live off?"

"We'll live off the bookshop. I'll sell pencils, books, paper. You can help me."

"Yes, I'll help you. When are we moving?"

"Tomorrow. Joseph is coming with his wagon."

Lucas and the child settle into Victor's house. Lucas repaints the rooms. They are light and clean. Lucas installs a bathroom in the small room next to the kitchen.

The child asks, "Can I have the skeletons?"

"Of course not. What if someone came into your room?"

"No one will come into my room. Except Yasmine when she comes back."

Lucas says, "All right. You can have the skeletons. But all the same we'll hide them behind a curtain."

Lucas and the child clear the garden, which was neglected by Victor. The child points to a tree.

"Look at that tree, Lucas. It's completely black."

Lucas says, "It's a dead tree. It should be cut down. The other trees are losing their leaves, but that one is dead."

Often in the middle of the night the child wakes up, rushes into Lucas's room, into his bed, and if Lucas isn't there, he waits for him in order to tell him his nightmares. Lucas lies down next to the child, and holds his little, thin body tightly until the child stops trembling.

The child tells him his nightmares, always the same ones, which recur regularly to haunt his nights.

One of these dreams is the river dream. The child, lying on the surface of the water, lets himself be carried off by the stream while watching the stars. The child is happy, but slowly something approaches, something frightening, and suddenly that thing, the child doesn't know what it is, explodes and screams and howls and blinds.

Another dream is the dream of the tiger lying next to the child's bed. The tiger appears to be asleep; it seems soft and gentle, and the child has a great desire to stroke it. The child is afraid, but his desire to stroke the tiger grows and the child can no longer resist this desire. His fingers touch the tiger's silky fur, and the tiger, with a swipe of its paw, rips his arm off.

Another dream is the dream of the desert island. The child is there playing with his wheelbarrow. He fills it with sand, transports the sand somewhere else, empties it again, and so on, for a long time. Then suddenly it is dark, it is cold, there is no one, anywhere, only the stars shine in their infinite solitude.

Another dream. The child wants to go back to Grandmother's house. He walks in the streets, but he does not know the streets in the town. He gets lost, the streets are deserted, the house is no longer where it should be, nothing is in the right place, Yasmine is calling for him, she is crying, but the child does not know which street, which alley to take in order to find her.

The most terrible dream is the dream of the dead tree, the black tree in the garden. The child is looking at the tree and the tree stretches out its bare branches toward the child. The tree says, "I am nothing but a dead tree, but I love you just as much as I did when I was alive." The tree speaks with Yasmine's voice, the child approaches, and the blackened, dead branches embrace him and strangle him.

Lucas chops down the dead tree, he saws it up and makes a bonfire in the garden.

When the fire goes out, the child says, "Now it is nothing but a pile of ashes."

He goes to his room. Lucas uncorks a bottle of brandy. He drinks. He is overcome with nausea. He goes back into the garden and he throws up. A plume of white smoke still rises from the black ashes, but then large raindrops begin to fall, and the shower finishes off the work of the fire.

Later, the child finds Lucas in the wet grass, in the mud. He shakes him.

"Get up, Lucas. You have to come in. It's raining. It's dark. It's cold. Can you walk?"

Lucas says, "Leave me here. Go inside. Tomorrow everything will be all right."

The child sits down next to Lucas; he waits.

The sun rises. Lucas opens his eyes.

"What happened, Mathias?"

The child says, "It's just a new nightmare."

5

The insomniac continues to appear at his window every evening at ten o'clock. The child is already in bed. Lucas leaves the house. The insomniac asks him the time, Lucas tells him. Then he goes to Clara's house. At dawn, when he comes home, the insomniac asks him the time again; Lucas tells him and goes to bed. A few hours later the light goes out in the insomniac's room and the pigeons take over his windowsill.

One morning, when Lucas comes home, the insomniac calls out, "Excuse me!"

Lucas says, "It is five o'clock."

"I know. I'm not interested in the time. It's just my way of starting a conversation with people. I just wanted to tell you that the child was very restless last night. He woke up about two o'clock, he went into your bedroom several times, he spent ages looking out the window. He even went out into the street, down to the bar, then he came back and went to bed, I suppose."

"Does he do that often?"

"He often wakes up, yes. Nearly every night. But it's the first time I've seen him leave the house during the night."

"Even during the day he never leaves the house."

"I think he was looking for you."

Lucas goes up to the apartment. The child is sleeping soundly in his bed. Lucas looks out the window. The insomniac asks, "Everything in order?"

"Yes. He's asleep. What about you? Do you never sleep?"

"I doze off now and again, but I never really sleep. I haven't slept for eight years."

"What do you do during the day?"

"I go for walks. When I feel tired I go and sit in a park. I spend most of my time in parks. It's there that I sometimes doze off for a few minutes, sitting on a bench. Would you like to come with me sometime?"

Lucas says, "Now, if you like."

"Fine. I'll feed my pigeons and come right down."

They walk down the deserted streets of the sleeping town toward Grandmother's house. The insomniac stops by a few square meters of yellow grass with two old trees spreading out their bare branches.

"Here's my park. The only place I can manage a moment's sleep."

The old man sits on the solitary bench next to a dried-up fountain covered in moss and mildew.

Lucas says, "There are nicer parks in town."

"Not for me."

He lifts his walking stick and points to large, beautiful house. "We used to live there, my wife and I."

"Is she dead?"

"She was killed by several shots from a revolver three years after the end of the war. One evening at ten o'clock."

Lucas sits down next to the old man.

"I remember her. We used to live by the border. When we came home from town we used to stop here to have a drink of water and rest. When your wife saw us from her window she would come down and bring us large lumps of potato sugar. I've never eaten it since. I remember her smile and her accent, and also her murder. The whole town talked about it."

"What did they say?"

"They said she was killed so they could nationalize the three textile factories that belonged to her."

The old man says, "She inherited those factories from her father. I worked there as an engineer. I married her and she stayed here. She loved this town very much. But she retained her nationality, and they were forced to kill her. It was the only solution. They killed her in our bedroom. I heard the gunshots from the bathroom. The assassin got in and out by the balcony. She was shot in the head, the chest, and the stomach. The inquiry concluded that it was an embittered employee who did it for revenge and then fled across the border."

Lucas says, "The border was already sealed, even then, and a worker wouldn't have owned a revolver."

The insomniac closes his eyes; he is silent.

Lucas asks, "Do you know who is living in your house now?"

"It's full of children. Our house has been turned into an orphanage. But you must get back, Lucas. Mathias will soon be waking up and you must open the bookshop."

"You're right. It's already half past seven."

* * *

Sometimes Lucas goes back to the park to chat with the insomniac. The old man talks about the past, about the happy times with his wife.

"She was always laughing. She was happy, carefree as a child. She loved the fruits, the flowers, the stars, the clouds. At sunset she would go out onto the balcony to look at the sky. She claimed that nowhere else in the world were sunsets as wonderful as in this town, were the colors in the sky so brilliant and beautiful."

The man closes his bloodshot eyes, heavy with sleeplessness. He continues in a different tone of voice, "After her murder, the authorities requisitioned the house and everything in it: all my wife's furniture, crockery, books, jewelry, clothes. All they let me take away was a suitcase with a few clothes. They told me I should leave town. I lost my job at the factory. I had no work, no house, and no money.

"I went to see a friend, a doctor, the same one I telephoned the night of the murder. He gave me some money for a train ticket. He said, 'Never come back to this town. It's a wonder they let you live.'

"I took the train, I arrived in the next town. I sat down in the waiting room in the station. I still had enough money to go farther, maybe even to the capital. But there was nothing for me to do in the capital, or in any other town. I bought a ticket at the booking office and came back here. I knocked at the door of a small house opposite the bookshop. I knew all the workers in our factories. I knew the woman who opened the door. She didn't ask any questions. She told me to come in, she led me to a room. 'You can stay here as long as you like, sir.'

"She is an old woman, she lost her husband, her two sons, and her daughter during the war. Her daughter was only seventeen.

She died at the front, where she had signed up as a nurse after being disfigured in a horrible accident. My landlady never speaks about it, and in fact she hardly speaks at all anymore. She leaves me alone in my room, which looks out onto the street. She herself lives in a smaller room which looks out onto the garden. The kitchen is also in back. I can use it when I want, and there is always something hot on the stove. Every morning I find my shoes polished, my shirts washed and ironed, lying over the back of a chair in the corridor outside my door. My landlady never comes into my room, and I see her rarely. We don't keep the same hours. I don't know what she lives on. On her war widow's pension and her garden, I suppose.

"A few months after I moved in I went to the council office to look for any sort of work. The officials sent me from one office to another. They were afraid to make a decision about me, I was an object of suspicion because of my marriage to a foreigner. Finally, it was the Party Secretary, Peter, who took me on as a handyman. I was a caretaker, a window cleaner, a sweeper of dust, dead leaves, and snow. Thanks to Peter I am now entitled to a retirement pension like everyone else. I didn't have to beg, and I can end my days in the town where I was born and where I have spent my whole life.

"I left my first wages on the kitchen table. It was a paltry amount, but to my landlady it was a lot of money, too much, according to her. She left half of it on the table, and we went on like that: I leave my small pension next to her plate every month; she leaves exactly half of it next to mine."

A woman wrapped in a large shawl comes out of the orphanage. She is thin and pale; her huge eyes shine in her bony face. She stops in front of the bench, looks at Lucas, smiles, and says to the old man, "I see you've found yourself a friend."

"Yes, a friend. This is Lucas, Judith. He runs the bookshop in the main square. Judith is in charge of the orphanage."

Lucas gets up. Judith shakes his hand.

"I should buy some books for the children, but I'm overwhelmed with work and my budget is very tight."

Lucas says, "I can send some books around with Mathias. How old are your children?"

"Between five and ten. Who is Mathias?"

The old man says, "Lucas is looking after an orphan."

Lucas says, "Mathias isn't an orphan. His mother has gone away. He's mine now."

Judith smiles. "My children aren't all orphans either. Mostly their fathers are unknown and they have been abandoned by their mothers, who are rape victims or prostitutes."

She sits down next to the old man, rests her head on his shoulder, closes her eyes.

"We'll need the heating soon, Michael. If the weather doesn't change we'll start the stoves on Monday."

The old man holds her close to him.

"Fine, Judith. I'll be there at five o'clock on Monday morning."

Lucas looks at the woman and the man, holding each other tight, their eyes closed, in the damp cold of an autumn morning, in the complete silence of a forgotten little town. He starts to tiptoe away, but Judith shivers, opens her eyes, gets up.

"Stay, Lucas. The children will be waking up. I have to make their breakfast." She kisses the old man on the forehead.

"Until Monday, Michael. See you, Lucas, and thanks in advance for the books."

She goes back to the house. Lucas sits down again.

"She is very beautiful."

"Very beautiful, yes." The insomniac laughs. "At first, she was suspicious of me. She saw me here every day, sitting on this bench. Maybe she took me for a pervert. One day she came and sat next to me and asked me what I was doing here. I told her everything. It was at the beginning of last winter. She asked me to help her with the heating in the rooms, she couldn't manage it alone, she only has a sixteen-year-old to help in the kitchen. There's no central heating in the building, just stoves in each room, seven of them. If you only knew what joy I felt to be able to go back into our house, our rooms! And also to be able to help Judith. She's had her trials. Her husband disappeared during the war, she herself was deported, she's been to hell and back. I mean that literally. There was a real fire behind those doors, lit by human beings to burn the bodies of other human beings."

Lucas says, "I know what you're talking about. I saw things like that with my own eyes, right here in this town."

"You must have been very young."

"I was no more than a child. But I forgot nothing."

"You will forget. Life is like that. Everything goes in time. Memories blur, pain diminishes. I remember my wife as one remembers a bird or a flower. She was the miracle of life in a world where everything seemed light, easy, and beautiful. At first I came here for her, now I come for Judith, the survivor. This might seem ridiculous to you, Lucas, but I'm in love with Judith. With her strength, her goodness, her kindness toward these children who aren't hers."

Lucas says, "I don't think it's ridiculous."

"At my age?"

"Age is irrelevant. The essential things matter. You love her and she loves you as well."

"She's waiting for her husband to return."

"Many women are waiting for or mourning their husbands who are disappeared or dead. But you just said, 'Pain diminishes, memories blur.' "

The insomniac raises his eyes to Lucas.

"Diminish, blur, I said, not disappear."

That same morning, Lucas picks out some children's books. He puts them in a box and says to Mathias, "Can you take these books to the orphanage next to the park on the way to Grandmother's house? It's a big house with a balcony, there's a fountain in front."

The child says, "I know the one."

"The principal is called Judith. Give her these books from me."

The child goes off with the books, but returns soon after. Lucas asks, "What did you think of Judith and the children?"

"I didn't see Judith and the children. I left the books outside the door."

"You didn't go in?"

"No. Why should I go in? So they can keep me?"

"What? What are you saying, Mathias!"

The child locks himself in his room. Lucas stays in the bookshop until closing time, then makes the evening meal, which he eats alone. He has a shower and is just getting dressed when the child comes quickly out of his room.

"Are you going out, Lucas? Where do you go to every evening?"

Lucas says, "I go to work. You know that."

The child lies on Lucas's bed. "I'll wait for you here. If you worked in the bars you would come home at closing time, at midnight. But you come home much later."

Lucas sits on a chair in front of the child. "Yes, Mathias, you're right. I do come home later. I go and see some friends after the bars close."

"Which friends?"

"You don't know them."

The child says, "I'm alone every night."

"You should be asleep at night."

"I would sleep if I knew you were here, in your room, asleep as well."

Lucas lies down next to the child. He kisses him.

"Did you really think I sent you to the orphanage so that they could keep you? How could you think such a thing?"

"I didn't really think that. But when I arrived at the door, I was afraid. You never know. Yasmine promised she would never leave me. Don't send me there again. I don't like going toward Grandmother's house."

Lucas says, "I understand."

The child says, "Orphans are children who don't have any parents. I don't have any parents."

"You do. You have your mother, Yasmine."

"Yasmine is gone. And what about my father? Where is he?"

"I'm your father."

"But the other one, the real one?"

Lucas is silent for a moment before replying, "He died before you were born, in an accident, like mine."

"Fathers always die in an accident. Will you have an accident too?"

"No. I'll be careful."

Lucas and the child work in the bookshop. The child takes books out of a box and hands them to Lucas, who is standing on a stepladder setting them on the shelves of the bookcase. It is a rainy autumn morning.

Peter comes into the shop. He is carrying a hooded falcon. The rain is dripping down his face onto the floor. From under his falcon he takes a packet wrapped up in jute cloth.

"Here, Lucas. I've brought them back. I can't keep them. It's not safe at my house anymore."

Lucas says, "You look pale, Peter. What happened?"

"Don't you read the newspapers? Don't you listen to the radio?"

"I never read newspapers and I only listen to old records."

Peter turns to the child. "Is this Yasmine's child?"

Lucas says, "Yes, this is Mathias. Say hello to Peter, Mathias. He's a friend."

Mathias stares at Peter in silence.

Peter says, "Mathias has already said hello with his eyes."

Lucas says, "Go and feed the animals, Mathias."

The child lowers his eyes, rummages about in the box of books. "It isn't time to feed the animals."

Lucas says, "You're right. Stay here and tell me if a customer comes in. Let's go upstairs, Peter."

They go up to Lucas's room.

Peter says, "That child has amazing eyes."

"Yes, he has Yasmine's eyes."

Peter gives Lucas the packet.

"There are pages missing from your notebooks, Lucas."

"I know, Peter. As I said, I make corrections, I cross things out. I delete anything that isn't indispensable."

"You correct, you cross out, you delete. Your brother Claus won't understand a word."

"Claus will understand."

"I understood too."

"Is that why you brought them back? Because you think you understood everything?"

Peter says, "What happened has nothing to do with your notebooks, Lucas. It's more serious than that. Our country is in the throes of an uprising. A counterrevolution. It began with intellectuals writing things they shouldn't have. Then it was taken up by the students. Students are always willing to sow the seeds of unrest. They organized a demonstration that degenerated into a riot against the forces of order. But it all began to get out of hand when the workers and even a part of the army joined up with the students. Yesterday evening, soldiers were distributing arms to irresponsible individuals. There are people shooting at each other in the capital, and it's now spreading to the provinces and the peasants."

Lucas says, "That covers every level of society."

"Except one. The class I belong to."

"You are greatly outnumbered by those who are against you."

"Indeed. But we have powerful friends."

Lucas is silent. Peter opens the door.

"We probably won't see each other again, Lucas. Let's part on good terms."

Lucas asks, "Where are you going?"

"Party officials have to place themselves under the protection of the foreign army."

Lucas gets up, holds Peter by the shoulders, and looks him in the eyes.

"Tell me, Peter! Aren't you ashamed?"

Peter grabs Lucas's hands and presses them to his face. He closes his eyes and says quietly, "Yes, Lucas. I am very ashamed." Tears escape from his closed eyes.

Lucas says, "No. Stop that. Get hold of yourself."

Lucas accompanies Peter to the street. He watches the dark silhouette walking away in the rain, head lowered, toward the station.

When Lucas comes back to the bookshop, the child says to him, "He's handsome. When is he coming back?"

"I don't know, Mathias. Maybe never."

That evening, Lucas goes to Clara's. He goes into the house, where all the lights are out. Clara's bed is cold and empty. Lucas lights the bedside lamp. On the pillow is a note from Clara: "I have gone to avenge Thomas."

Lucas goes home. He finds the child in his bed. He says, "I'm sick of finding you in my bed every night. Go to your room and get some sleep."

The child's lip trembles. He sniffs. "I heard Peter say that people are shooting at each other in the capital. Do you think Yasmine is in danger?"

"Yasmine isn't in danger, don't worry."

"You said that Peter might never come back. Do you think he'll die?"

"No, I don't think so. But Clara, definitely."

"Who's Clara?"

"A friend. Go to bed, Mathias, and sleep. I'm very tired."

In the little town hardly anything happens. The foreign flags are removed from public buildings, along with the effigies of Party officials. A parade passes through town with the old national flags, singing the old national anthem and other old songs, recalling another revolution in another century.

The bars are packed. People talk, laugh, sing louder than usual.

Lucas listens to the radio continually, until the day when classical music replaces the news broadcast.

Lucas looks out the window. In the main square stands a foreign army tank.

Lucas goes out to buy a pack of cigarettes. All the shops are closed. He has to go to the railway station. He passes other tanks along the way. The gun barrels turn in his direction, track him. The streets are deserted, the windows are shut, the shutters closed. But the station and the surrounding area are full of soldiers and border guards without weapons. Lucas approaches one of them: "What's going on?"

"I don't know. We've been demobilized. Did you want to catch a train? There are no trains for civilians."

"I didn't want to catch a train. I just wanted to buy some cigarettes. The shops are closed."

The soldier hands Lucas a pack of cigarettes. "You're not allowed inside the station. Take this pack and go home. It's dangerous out on the streets."

Lucas goes home. The child is still awake; they listen to the radio together. Lots of music and a few short speeches. "We have won the revolution. The people are victorious. Our government has asked for the help of our great protectors against the enemies of the people." And again: "Remain calm. Gatherings of more than two people are forbidden. The sale of alcohol is forbidden. Restaurants and bars will remain closed until further notice. All individual journeys by train or bus are forbidden. Observe the curfew. Do not leave the house after nightfall."

More music, then instructions and threats: "Work must begin again in the factories. Any workers who do not turn up at their place of work will be laid off. Saboteurs will be brought up before special tribunals. They will face the death sentence."

The child says, "I don't understand. Who won the revolution? And why is everything forbidden? Why are they so evil?"

Lucas switches off the radio. "We won't listen to the radio anymore. There's no point."

There is still some resistance, fighting, strikes. There are also arrests, imprisonments, disappearances, executions. Two hundred thousand panic-stricken inhabitants leave the country.

A few months later, silence, calm, and order reign once more.

Lucas rings at Peter's door. "I know you're back. Why are you hiding from me?"

"I'm not hiding from you. I just thought you wouldn't want to see me. I was waiting for you to make the first move."

Lucas laughs. "I've made it. Basically, things are just like before. The revolution has achieved nothing."

Peter says, "History will be the judge of that."

Lucas laughs again. "Such grand words. What's got into you, Peter?"

"Don't laugh. I've been through a serious crisis. First I resigned from the Party, then I let myself be persuaded into taking up my old position in this town. I like this town very much. It has a hold on my soul. Once you've lived here you can't not come back. And besides, Lucas, there's you."

"Is that a declaration of love?"

"No. Of friendship. I know I can't expect anything from you on that score. What about Clara? Has she come back?"

"No, Clara hasn't come back. Someone else has already moved into her house."

Peter says, "There were thirty thousand deaths in the capital. They even fired on a march where there were women and children. If Clara participated in anything . . ."

"She certainly participated in everything that was going on in the capital. I think she has rejoined Thomas, and that is for the best. She never stopped talking about Thomas. She thought only of Thomas, loved only Thomas, was ill because of Thomas. One way or another she would have died for Thomas."

After a silence, Peter says, "Many people crossed the border during the troubled period when it was left unguarded. Why didn't you take advantage of it to rejoin your brother?"

"I didn't consider it for a moment. How could I leave the child all on his own?"

"You could have taken him with you."

"You don't set off on an adventure like that with a child his age."

"You can set off anywhere, anytime, with whoever you want, if you want to badly enough. The child is just an excuse."

Lucas lowers his head. "The child has to stay here. He's waiting for his mother to come back. He wouldn't have come with me."

Peter doesn't answer. Lucas raises his head and looks at him. "You're right. I don't want to go find Claus. It's up to him to come back. He's the one who went away."

Peter says, "Someone who doesn't exist can't come back."

"Claus exists and he will come back!"

Peter goes up to Lucas and grabs him by the shoulder. "Calm down. You have to face facts. Neither your brother nor the child's mother will ever come back, and you know it."

Lucas mumbles, "Claus will."

He falls forward off his chair, he hits his head on the edge of the low table; he slumps onto the carpet. Peter pulls him onto the sofa, he wets a cloth and wipes Lucas's face, which is bathed in sweat. When Lucas comes to, Peter gives him a drink and lights him a cigarette.

"I'm sorry, Lucas. We won't talk about this again."

Lucas asks, "What were we talking about?"

"What about?" Peter lights another cigarette. "About politics, of course."

Lucas laughs. "It must have been pretty boring for me to fall asleep on your sofa."

"Yes, that's right, Lucas. You've always found politics boring, haven't you?"

The child is six and a half. On the first day of school Lucas wants to accompany him, but the child prefers to go on his own. When he comes home at noon, Lucas asks him whether everything went all right. The child says that everything went all right.

In the days that follow the child says that everything is going well at school. But one day he returns with a wound on his cheek. He says that he fell. Another day his right hand bears some red marks. The next day the nails on this hand all turn black, with the exception of the thumbnail. The child says that he jammed his fingers in a door. For weeks afterward, he has to write with his left hand.

One evening the child comes home with his mouth all split and swollen. He is unable to eat. Lucas doesn't ask questions, he pours some milk into the child's mouth, then places a sock filled with sand, a pointed stone, and a razor on the table. He says, "These were our weapons when we had to defend ourselves against the other children. Take them. Defend yourself!"

The child says, "There were two of you. I'm on my own."

"Even on your own you have to learn how to defend yourself."

The child looks at the objects on the table. "I can't. I could never hit anyone, hurt anyone."

"Why not? They hit you and hurt you."

The child looks Lucas in the eyes.

"Physical wounds don't matter when I receive them. But if I had to inflict them on someone else, that would wound me in a way I couldn't bear."

Lucas asks, "Do you want me to talk to your teacher?"

The child says, "Definitely not! I forbid it! Don't ever do that, Lucas! Have I complained? Have I asked for your help? Your weapons?"

He sweeps the defensive tools off the table. "I'm stronger than all of them, braver, and above all, more intelligent. That's all that matters."

Lucas throws the stone and the sock full of sand into the garbage. He closes the razor, puts it in his pocket. "I still carry it on me, but I don't use it anymore."

When the child has gone to bed, Lucas goes into his room and sits down on the edge of his bed. "I won't meddle in your affairs any more, Mathias. I won't ask any more questions. When you want to leave school, just tell me."

The child says, "I'll never leave school."

Lucas asks, "Tell me, Mathias, do you cry sometimes when you're alone?"

The child says, "I'm used to being alone. I never cry, you know that."

"Yes, I know. But you never laugh either. When you were small you laughed all the time."

"That must have been before Yasmine died."

"What are you saying, Mathias? Yasmine isn't dead."

"She is dead. I've known for a long time. Otherwise she would have come back."

After a silence, Lucas says, "Even after Yasmine left, you still laughed, Mathias."

The child looks at the ceiling. "Yes, maybe. Before we left Grandmother's house. We should never have left Grandmother's house."

Lucas takes the child's face in his hands. "Perhaps you're right. Perhaps we shouldn't have left Grandmother's house."

The child closes his eyes. Lucas kisses him on the forehead. "Sleep well, Mathias. When you feel too much pain, too much sorrow, and you don't want to talk to anyone, write it down. It will help you."

The child answers, "I've already written it down. I've written down everything. Everything that has happened since we've been here. My nightmares, the school, everything. I've got a big notebook like you. You've got lots, I've only got one, only a slim one so far. I'll never let you read it. You forbade me to read yours, I forbid you to read mine."

At ten o'clock in the morning an old bearded man comes into the bookshop. Lucas has seen him before. He is one of his best customers. Lucas gets up and asks with a smile, "What can I do for you, sir?"

"I have everything I need, thank you. I came to talk to you about Mathias. I'm his teacher. I have written to you on numerous occasions to ask you to come and see me."

Lucas says, "I never received your letters."

"Yet you've signed them."

The teacher takes three envelopes from his pocket and hands them to Lucas. "Isn't that your signature?"

Lucas examines the letters. "Yes and no. It's a good forgery of my signature."

The teacher smiles as he takes back the letters. "That's the conclusion I came to also. Mathias doesn't want me to speak with you. I decided to come and see you during school hours. I left an older pupil in charge of the class during my absence. This visit can remain our secret, if you wish."

Lucas says, "Yes, I think that would be best. Mathias has forbidden me to talk to you."

"He's very proud, arrogant even. He is also by far the most intelligent pupil in the class. Nevertheless, the only advice I can offer you is to withdraw him from school. I can sign the necessary papers."

Lucas says, "Mathias doesn't want to leave school."

"If only you knew what he goes through! The cruelty of the other children is beyond belief. The girls make fun of him. They call him 'spider,' 'hunchback,' 'bastard.' He sits on his own in the front row, no one wants to sit next to him. The boys hit him, kick him, punch him. The boy behind him slammed the desk shut on his fingers. I have intervened many times, but that just aggravates the situation. The other children can't stand the fact that Mathias knows everything, that he's best at everything. They are jealous of him and they are making his life unbearable."

Lucas says, "I know it, even though he never talks to me."

"No, he never complains. He doesn't even cry. He has considerable strength of character. But he can't go on suffering so much humiliation forever. Withdraw him from school and I will come every evening to give him lessons here. It would be a real pleasure for me to work with such a gifted child."

Lucas says, "Thank you, but it's not up to me. Mathias insists on going to school normally, like the other children. For him, leaving school would mean recognizing his difference, his infirmity."

The teacher says, "I understand. However, he *is* different, and one day he will have to accept it."

Lucas is silent. The teacher browses through the books on the shelves.

"These premises are very spacious. What would you say to setting out a few tables and chairs to make a reading room for the children? I could bring you some secondhand books, I've got plenty that I don't know what to do with. Then the children whose parents don't own books, and there are lots of them, believe me, could come and read in peace here for an hour or two."

Lucas stares at the teacher. "You think that might improve the relations between Mathias and the other children, don't you? Yes, it's worth a try. It's probably a good idea."

6

It is ten o'clock at night. Peter rings at Lucas's house. Lucas throws him the front-door key from the window. Peter comes up and enters the room. "Am I disturbing you?"

"Not at all. On the contrary. I was looking for you, but you had disappeared. Even Mathias was worried about you."

Peter says, "That's nice. Is he asleep?"

"He's in his room, but how do I know if he's asleep or doing something else? He wakes up at all hours of the night and starts reading, writing, thinking, studying."

"Can he hear us?"

"He can if he wants to, yes."

"In that case I'd rather you came to my place."

"Fine."

At his house, Peter opens the windows in all the rooms. He collapses into an armchair. "This heat is unbearable. Fix yourself a drink and sit down. I've just come from the station. I've been traveling all day. I had to change trains four times and wait ages for the connections."

Lucas pours a drink. "Where have you been?"

"To my hometown. I was summoned there by the local magistrate concerning Victor. He strangled his sister in a fit of *delirium tremens.*"

Lucas says, "Poor Victor. Did you see him?"

"Yes, I saw him. He's in an insane asylum."

"How is he?"

"Very well, very calm. His face is a bit puffed up because of the medication he's on. He was happy to see me. He asked about you, and the shop, and the child. He sends his greetings."

"And what did he say about his sister?"

"He said quietly, 'It's done now, we can't change it.' "

Lucas asks, "What will become of him?"

"I don't know. They haven't had the trial yet. I think he'll spend the rest of his days in the asylum. Victor doesn't belong in a prison. I asked if there was anything I could do for him. He said to send him a regular supply of writing materials. 'Paper and pencils are all I need. Here I can finally write my book,' he said."

"Yes, Victor wanted to write a book. He told me when I bought the bookshop. In fact, that's the reason he sold it."

"Yes, and he's already started writing." Peter takes a pile of typewritten sheets from his briefcase. "I read them on the train. Take them home, read them, and bring them back to me. He typed them next to his sister's body. He strangled his sister and then sat at his desk to write. They were found like that, in Victor's room, the sister strangled, stretched out on the bed, Victor typing, drinking brandy, smoking cigars. It was some of his sister's clients who called the police the next day. On the day of the crime, Victor left the house, drew some money from the bank, went to buy some brandy, cigarettes, and cigars. He told the clients who had an appointment for a fitting and were waiting outside the door that his sister was feeling poorly because of the heat and didn't want to be disturbed. The clients, obstinate and no doubt impatient to have their new dresses, came back the next day, knocked at the door, spoke to the neighbors, decided that the whole thing was a bit strange, and finally went to contact the police. The police forced the door open and found Victor blind drunk, quietly typing away at his manuscript. He let himself be led away without resistance, taking the finished sheets along with him. Read them. There are a lot of errors, but they're readable, and very interesting."

Lucas goes home with Victor's manuscript and starts to copy it out into his notebook during the night:

It is August 15; the heat wave has lasted three weeks now. The heat is unbearable indoors as well as outside. You can't get away from it. I don't like the heat, I don't like summer. A wet, cool summer, fine, but these dog days have always made me feel positively ill.

I have just strangled my sister. She is lying on my bed. I have covered her with a sheet. In this heat her body will soon start smelling. No matter. I'll report it later. I've locked the front door, and if anyone knocks I won't answer. I've also closed the windows and pulled the shutters.

I've lived with my sister for almost two years. I sold the bookshop and house I owned in a little town far away near the border. I came to live with my sister in order to write a book. I thought I would be unable to do it in the little town far away because of the solitude that threatened to make me ill and turn me into an alcoholic. I thought that here, with my sister taking care of the housework, the meals, and the clothes, I would lead a healthy, regular life, which would at last allow me to write the book that I've always wanted to write.

Unfortunately, the calm and quiet life I'd anticipated quickly turned into hell on earth.

My sister watched over me, spied on me constantly. Right from my arrival she forbade me to drink or smoke, and whenever I returned from an errand or a walk she would kiss me affectionately, solely, I realized, in order to detect the smell of drink or tobacco on my breath.

I abstained from drink for several months, but I was quite incapable of giving up smoking as well. I smoked in secret like a schoolboy. I would buy a cigar or a pack of cigarettes and go off for a walk in the forest. On the way back I would chew pine needles or suck mints to get rid of the smell. I also smoked at night with the window open, even in winter.

Many times I sat down at my desk with some sheets of paper, but my mind was a complete blank.

What could I write about? Nothing happened in my life, nothing ever had happened in my life or in the world around me. Nothing worth writing about. And my sister disturbed me all the time; she came into my room on the slightest pretext. She brought me tea, dusted the furniture, put away my clean clothes in the wardrobe. She would also lean over my shoulder to see how my writing was coming along. Because of this I had to fill in sheet after sheet, and since I didn't know what to write on them, I copied out excerpts from books, any books. Sometimes my sister would read a phrase over my shoulder that pleased her, and would encourage me with a contented smile.

There was no chance of her seeing through my deceit, for she never read herself; she possibly never read a book in her life. She never had the time—since childhood she has worked from morning till night.

In the evening she made me come into the sitting room. "You've worked enough for one day. Let's chat for a while."

As she talked, she did her sewing, either by hand or on her old pedal-driven sewing machine. She talked about her neighbors, her clients, about dresses and fabrics, about how tired she felt, and all the sacrifices she had made to ensure the success of the work of her brother, me, Victor.

I had to sit there, without being able to smoke or drink, listening to this drivel. When finally she went to her room, I went to my own, lit a cigar or a cigarette, picked up a sheet of paper, and filled it with insults directed at my sister, her narrow-minded clients, and her stupid dresses. I hid the sheet among the others containing random excerpts from some book or other.

For Christmas my sister gave me a typewriter.

"Your manuscript is already quite thick. You'll soon be reaching the end of your book, I imagine. Then you'll need to type it up. You took typing lessons at business school, and even if you've forgotten some of it through lack of practice you'll soon pick it up again."

I was in the depths of despair, but in order to please my sister I sat down straight away at my desk and, somewhat clumsily, began copying out various pages, themselves copied from some book or other. My sister watched me, nodding her head with satisfaction.

"You're not too bad at it, Victor. I'm surprised, you're actually quite good. You'll soon be typing as quickly as you used to."

When I was alone, I reread what I had typed. It was nothing but a series of typing errors and misprints.

A few days later, on my way back from my "constitutional," I went into a local bar. I only wanted a cup of tea to warm myself up a bit, for my hands and feet were cold and completely numb because of my poor circulation. I sat at a table next to the stove, and when the waiter asked me what I wanted I said, "Tea." Then I added, "With some rum in it."

I don't know why I said that; I didn't intend to say it, but I did nevertheless. I drank my tea with rum and ordered another rum, without the tea this time, and then a third rum after that.

I looked around anxiously. It isn't a big town, and almost everyone knows my sister. If she found out from one of her clients or neighbors that I'd been in a bar! But I saw only the faces of tired, indifferent, distracted men, and my anxiety subsided. I had another rum and left the bar. I was a bit unsure on my feet. I hadn't drunk for several months, and the alcohol had gone straight to my head.

I didn't dare go home. I was afraid of my sister. I wandered around the streets for a while, then I went into a shop to buy some mints. I put two in my mouth immediately. When I went to pay, without knowing why, without wanting to say it, I casually told the assistant, "I'll also have a bottle of plum brandy, two packs of cigarettes, and three cigars."

I put the bottle in the inside pocket of my overcoat. Outside it was snowing. I felt perfectly happy. I was no longer afraid of going home, no longer afraid of my sister. When I arrived back at the house she called out from the room which serves as her workshop. "I've got a rush job, Victor. Your supper is in the oven. I'll eat later."

I ate quickly in the kitchen, retired to my room, and locked the door. It was the first time I had dared to lock my door. When my sister tried to come into my room, I shouted, I dared to shout,

"Don't disturb me! I've had some brilliant ideas! I must get them on paper before I lose them."

My sister replied humbly, "I didn't want to disturb you. I just wanted to wish you good night."

"Good night, Sophie!"

She didn't leave.

"I had this very demanding client. She wanted her dress finished for the New Year. I'm sorry you had to eat on your own, Victor."

"It doesn't matter," I replied nicely. "Go to bed, Sophie, it's late."

After a silence she asked, "Why have you locked the door, Victor? You didn't need to lock it. That wasn't really necessary."

I drank a mouthful of brandy to calm myself. "I don't want to be disturbed. I'm writing."

"That's good. Very good, Victor."

I drank the bottle of brandy—it was only a half-liter—smoked two cigars and numerous cigarettes. I threw the butts out the window. It was still snowing. The snow covered the butts and the empty bottle, which I had also thrown out the window, out into the street.

The next morning my sister knocked at my door. I didn't answer. She knocked again. I shouted, "Let me sleep!"

I heard her go.

I didn't get up until two o'clock in the afternoon. My sister and her meal were waiting for me in the kitchen. This was our conversation:

"I reheated the meal three times."

"I'm not hungry. Make me some coffee."

"It's two o'clock. How can you sleep so long?"

"I was writing till five o'clock this morning. I am an artist. I have the right to work when I want, whenever I feel inspired. Writing is not the same as sewing. Get that into your head, Sophie."

My sister looked at me admiringly. "You're right, Victor, I'm sorry. Will it soon be finished, your book?"

"Yes, soon."

"How wonderful! It will be a very fine book, if the bits I've read are anything to go on."

I thought, "Stupid cow!"

I drank more and more; I became careless. I left packs of cigarettes in the pocket of my overcoat. My sister brushed and cleaned it in order to search the pockets. One day she came into my room brandishing a half-empty pack. "You're smoking!"

I answered defiantly, "Yes, I'm smoking. I can't write without smoking."

"You promised me you'd stop!"

"I also promised myself. But then I realized that I couldn't write if I didn't smoke. It was a moral dilemma, Sophie. If I stop smoking, I also stop writing. I decided that it was better to carry on smoking and writing than to live without writing. I've nearly finished my book. You should leave me in peace, Sophie, to finish my book and not worry about whether I smoke or not."

My sister was impressed by this. She went out and came back with an ashtray, which she placed on my desk.

"Go ahead and smoke. It's not so bad if it's for your book. . . ."

As for drinking, I adopted the following tactic. I bought liter bottles of brandy in different parts of town, taking care not to go into the same shop twice in a row. I would bring the bottle home in the inside pocket of my overcoat and hide it in the umbrella stand in the corridor, and when my sister went out or went to bed

I would grab the bottle, lock myself in my room, and smoke and drink late into the night.

I avoided bars, I came home sober from my walks, and everything was going fine between my sister and me until the spring of this year, when Sophie began to get impatient.

"Won't you ever finish that book, Victor? This can't go on. You never get up before two o'clock in the afternoon, you look terrible, you'll make yourself ill, and me besides."

"I've finished it, Sophie. I now have to correct it and type it up. It's a big job."

"I never thought it would take so much time to write a book."

"A book's not the same as a dress, Sophie, remember that."

Summer came. I suffered terribly from the heat. I spent the afternoons in the forest, lying under the trees. Sometimes I slept and had confused dreams. One day I was awakened by a storm, a huge storm. It was August 14. I left the forest as quickly as my bad leg would allow. I sought shelter in the first bar along the way. It was a workingmen's bar. Everyone was glad about the storm, as it hadn't rained for several months. I ordered a lemonade. They all laughed, and one of them offered me a glass of red wine. I accepted. Then I ordered a bottle and offered it around. And so we carried on as the rain continued to fall. I ordered one bottle after another. I felt exceptionally good, surrounded by this warm camaraderie. I spent all the money I had on me. My companions gradually drifted away, but I didn't want to go home. I felt alone; I didn't have a home to go to. I didn't know where to go. I would have liked to have gone back to my house, my bookshop, in the faraway little town that was my ideal place. I knew now, for certain, that I should never have left that border town to live with my sister, whom I had hated since childhood.

The bartender said, "Closing time!"

Out on the street my left leg, the bad one, gave out under me, and I fell over.

I don't remember the rest. I woke up bathed in sweat in my bed. I didn't dare leave my room. Slowly it all began to come back to me. The vulgar, laughing faces in a local bar . . . later, the rain, the mud . . . the uniforms of the policemen who brought me home . . . my sister's horrified expression . . . the insults I hurled at her . . . the policemen's laughter . . .

The house was silent. Outside, the sun was shining again; the heat was suffocating.

I got up, took my old suitcase from under the bed, and started packing my clothes. It was the only solution. Leave here as soon as possible. My head was spinning. My eyes, my mouth, my throat felt raw. I felt dizzy and had to sit down. I decided I would never make it to the station in this state. I rummaged around in the wastepaper basket, found a virtually full bottle of brandy. I drank from the bottle. I felt better. I touched the back of my head. I had a painful bump behind my left ear. I picked up the bottle, lifted it to my mouth, and my sister came into the room. I put the bottle down, and I waited. My sister also waited. There was a long silence. She finally broke it, speaking in a weird, calm voice.

"What have you got to say to me?"

"Nothing," I said.

She screamed, "It's so easy! It would be, wouldn't it! He's got nothing to say! He is picked up by the police, blind drunk, lying in the mud, and he has nothing to say!"

I said, "Let me be. I'm leaving."

She snorted, "So I see, you've packed your case. But where will you go, you stupid fool, where will you go without money?"

"I've still got some money in the bank from the sale of the bookshop."

"Oh, really? I ask myself how much money you have left. You sold off the bookshop for a pittance, and the little money you made from it you've squandered on drink and cigarettes."

Of course I had never told her about the gold and silver pieces and the jewelry I received as well, which were also deposited in the bank. I simply replied, "I've got enough left to go away."

She said, "And what about me? *I* haven't been paid. I've fed you, housed you, taken care of you. Who'll repay me for all that?"

I fastened up my case. "I'll pay you. Let me leave."

Suddenly much softer, she said, "Don't be childish, Victor. I'll give you a last chance. What happened yesterday evening was just an accident, a relapse. It will all be different when you've finished your book."

I asked, "What book?"

She picked up my "manuscript." "This book, your book."

"I didn't write a single word of it."

"There are nearly two hundred pages of typescript."

"Yes, two hundred pages copied from other books."

"Copied? I don't understand."

"You'll never understand anything. I copied these two hundred pages from books. I didn't write a single word of it."

She looked at me. I raised the bottle and drank. A long drink. She shook her head. "I don't believe you. You're drunk. You're talking nonsense. Why would you do that?"

I snickered. "To make you believe I was writing. You disturb me, you spy on me constantly, you prevent me from writing; seeing you, your very presence in this house, prevents me from writing. You destroy everything, degrade everything, annihilate all creativity, life, freedom, inspiration. Since childhood you've done nothing but watch over me, guide me, annoy me, since childhood!"

She remained silent for a moment, then she said, she recited, staring down at the floor, the threadbare carpet, "I sacrificed everything for your work, your book. My own work, my clients, my last years. I walked on tiptoe so as not to disturb you. And you haven't written a single word during the two years you've been here? You do nothing but eat, drink, and smoke! You're nothing but a good-for-nothing cheat, a drunk, and a parasite! I told all my clients that your book was about to appear! And you've written nothing? I'll be the laughingstock of the whole town! You've brought dishonor on my house! I should have left you wallowing in your dirty little town and your filthy bookshop. You lived there, alone, for more than twenty years, so why didn't you write a book there where I wasn't disturbing you, where no one was disturbing you? Why? Because you couldn't even write one word of a third-rate book, no matter where you were or how you were living."

I kept on drinking while she was talking, and then heard my own voice answer her from afar, as if coming from the next room. I told her she was right, that I wouldn't be able, was not able to write anything at all as long as she was still alive. I reminded her of our childhood sexual experiences, which she'd initiated, being older than me by several years, and which had shocked me more deeply than she could ever imagine.

My sister replied that they were just childish games, and that it was in bad taste to bring them up again, especially since she had remained a virgin and had had no interest in "that" for a long time.

I said I knew "that" didn't interest her, she was happy to stroke the hips and breasts of her clients, I had watched her during fittings, I'd seen the pleasure she took in touching her young clients, beautiful as she had never been; depraved was all she had ever been.

I told her that because of her ugliness and her hypocritical puritanism, she had never been able to interest any man. So she turned instead to her clients and used taking measurements and smoothing out the material as a pretext for touching the young, beautiful women who ordered dresses from her.

My sister said, "You're going too far, Victor. That's enough!"

She grabbed the bottle, my bottle of brandy, she smashed it over the typewriter, the brandy spilled out over the desk. My sister came toward me, holding the neck of the broken bottle.

I stood up, pinned her arm back, twisted her wrist; she dropped the bottle. We fell onto the bed, and I lay on top of her. I gripped her skinny throat in my hands, and when she stopped struggling, I ejaculated.

The next day Lucas takes Victor's manuscript back to Peter.

A few months later, Peter goes back to his hometown to take part in the trial. He is away for several weeks. On his return he calls in at the bookshop, strokes Mathias's hair, and says to Lucas. "Come and see me this evening."

Lucas says, "Sounds like bad news, Peter."

Peter shakes his head. "Don't ask any questions now. See you later."

When Peter leaves, the child turns to Lucas. "Has something bad happened to Peter?"

"Not to Peter, but to one of his friends, I'm afraid."

The child says, "It's the same thing, it's maybe even worse."

Lucas holds Mathias close. "You're right. Sometimes it's worse."

When he gets to Peter's, Lucas asks, "Well?"

Peter drinks the glass of brandy he has just poured in a single gulp. "Well? Sentenced to death. Executed yesterday by hanging. Drink up!"

"You're drunk, Peter!"

Peter raises the bottle, examines the level of the liquid, snickers. "You're right, I've already drunk half a bottle. I'm taking over where Victor left off."

Lucas gets up. "I'll come back another time. It's no use talking to you in this state."

Peter says, "On the contrary. I can't talk about Victor unless I'm in this state. Sit down. Here, this belongs to you. Victor sends it to you." He pushes a small linen bag over to Lucas.

Lucas asks, "What is it?"

"Gold coins and jewelry. Some money as well. Victor didn't have enough time to spend it. He said, 'Give this all back to Lucas. He paid too much for the house and the bookshop. As for you, Peter, I leave you my house, the house of my sister and our parents. We don't have any heirs, neither my sister nor I have an heir. Sell this house, it is cursed. It has had a curse on it since our childhood. Sell it, and go back to the little town far away, that wonderful place I never should have left.' "

After a silence, Lucas says, "You thought Victor would receive a lighter sentence. You even hoped he would avoid prison and live out his days in an asylum."

"I was wrong, that's all. I couldn't know that the psychiatrists would judge Victor responsible for his actions, nor that Victor would act like a fool at his trial. He showed no remorse, no regret, no contrition. He just kept on repeating, 'I had to do it, I had to kill her. It was the only way I could write my book.' The jury deemed that no one had a right to kill someone solely because that person was preventing him from writing a book. They also declared that it would be too easy to have a few drinks, kill an honest person, and get away with it. They concluded that Victor was a selfish, perverse individual who was a danger to society. Apart from me all the witnesses gave evidence against him in favor of his sister, who led an honorable, exemplary life, and was appreciated by everyone, particularly her clients."

Lucas asks, "Were you able to see him apart from the trial?"

"After the sentence, yes. I was allowed to go into his cell and stay as long as I wanted. I kept him company up to the end."

"Was he afraid?"

"Afraid? I don't think that's the right word. At first he didn't believe it, he couldn't believe it. Was he expecting a pardon, a miracle? I don't know. The day he wrote and signed his will he certainly had no illusions. The final evening he said to me, 'I know I'm going to die, Peter, but I don't understand it. Instead of just one corpse, my sister's, there will now be a second, mine. But who needs a second corpse? Certainly not God, he has no use for our bodies. Society? It would gain a book or two by letting me live, instead of gaining an extra corpse which would benefit no one.' "

Lucas asks, "Did you go to the execution?"

"No. He asked me to, but I said no. You think I'm a coward, don't you?"

"Not for the first time. But I understand."

"Would you have gone?"

"If he had asked me, yes, I would have gone."

7

The bookshop has been converted into a reading room. Some children have already got into the habit of going there to read or draw; others come in at random when they are cold or tired from having been out playing too long in the snow. These children stay a quarter of an hour or so, just long enough to get warm and flip through some picture books. There are also those who peer through the shop window and then run away when Lucas comes out to invite them in.

Now and then Mathias comes down from the apartment, sits down with a book next to Lucas, goes back up after an hour or two, and returns for closing time. He doesn't mix with the other children. When they have left, Mathias rearranges the books, empties the wastepaper basket, places the chairs on the tables, and wipes down the floor. He also keeps accounts: "They've stolen another seven colored pencils, three books, and they've wasted dozens of sheets of paper."

Lucas says, "It's nothing, Mathias. If they asked I'd give them these things for free. They're shy, they prefer to take things in secret. It's not important."

Late one afternoon, while everyone is reading in silence, Mathias slides a note to Lucas. It says, "Look at that woman!" Outside the window, in the darkness of the street, the shadowy figure of a woman, a faceless silhouette, is looking into the brightly lit bookshop. Lucas gets up and the shadow disappears.

Mathias whispers, "She follows me everywhere. At recess she watches me over the playground fence. She walks behind me on the way home from school."

Lucas asks, "Does she speak to you?"

"No. Once, a few days ago, she offered me an apple, but I didn't take it. Another time, when four other boys were holding me down in the snow and were about to undress me, she scolded them and hit them. I ran away."

"She's not evil, then. She defended you."

"Yes, but why? She has no reason to defend me. And why does she follow me? Why does she watch me? Her look scares me. Her eyes scare me."

Lucas says, "Don't pay any attention, Mathias. Many women lost their children during the war, so they get attached to another child who reminds them of the one they lost."

Mathias snickers. "I'd be surprised if I reminded anyone of her child."

That evening, Lucas rings at the door of Yasmine's aunt. She opens the window. "What do you want?"

"To talk to you."

"I haven't time. I have to go to work."

"I'll wait for you."

When she comes out of the house, Lucas says, "I'll walk with you. Do you often work at night?"

"One week in three. Like everybody else. What do you want to talk about? My job?"

"No. About the child. I just want to ask you to leave him alone."

"I've done nothing to him."

"I know. But you follow him, you watch him. It bothers him. Do you understand?"

"Yes. Poor little thing. She left him."

They walk silently down the empty, snow-covered street. The woman hides her face in her scarf; her shoulders shake with her silent sobbing.

Lucas asks, "When will your husband be freed?"

"My husband? He's dead. Didn't you know?"

"No. I'm sorry."

"Officially he committed suicide. But I heard from someone who knew him inside, who's now been released, that it wasn't suicide. It was his cellmates who killed him because of what he did to his daughter."

They reach the front of the large textile factory, which is lit up by neon lights. From all sides shivering, shadowy figures hurry in and disappear through the metal gate. Even out here the noise of the machines is deafening.

Lucas asks, "If your husband weren't dead, would you take him back?"

"I don't know. He wouldn't have dared come back to this town in any case. I think he would have gone to the capital to look for Yasmine."

The factory siren goes. Lucas says, "I'll let you go. You'll be late."

The woman raises her pale, youthful face; she has the brilliant, dark eyes of Yasmine.

"Now that I'm on my own, I could maybe, if you like, if you wanted, take the child in."

Lucas screams louder than the factory siren. "Take Mathias? Never! He's mine, mine alone! I forbid you to go near him, watch him, talk to him, or follow him!"

The woman retreats toward the factory gate. "Calm down. Have you gone mad? It was only a suggestion."

Lucas turns on his heels and runs back to the bookshop. He leans against the wall of the house and waits for his heartbeat to slow down.

A young girl enters the bookshop, comes up to Lucas, smiles.

"Don't you recognize me, Lucas?"

"Should I?"

"Agnes."

Lucas tries to think. "I'm sorry, Miss, I don't recall."

"But we're old friends. I once came to your house to listen to music. I suppose I was only six at the time. You wanted to make me a swing."

Lucas says, "I remember. Your Aunt Leonie sent you."

"That's right. She's dead now. This time it's the factory manager who sent me to buy some picture books for the children in the day-care center."

"You work at the factory? You should still be at school."

Agnes blushes. "I'm fifteen. I left school last year. I don't work at the factory, I'm a kindergarten teacher. The children call me Miss."

Lucas laughs. "I called you Miss as well."

She hands Lucas a bill. "Give me some books, and also some paper and pencils for drawing."

Agnes comes by often. She browses at length among the books

on the shelves, she sits with the children, she reads and draws with them.

The first time that Mathias sees her he says to Lucas, "She's a very beautiful woman."

"A woman? She's just a kid."

"She's got breasts, she's not a kid anymore."

Lucas looks at Agnes's breasts, enhanced by a red sweater.

"You're right, Mathias, she does have breasts. I hadn't noticed."

"What about her hair? She has lovely hair. Look how it shines in the light."

Lucas looks at Agnes's long blond hair shining in the light.

Mathias continues, "Look at her dark eyelashes."

Lucas says, "It's eyeshadow."

"Her mouth."

"Lipstick. At her age she shouldn't be wearing makeup."

"You're right, Lucas. She'd be beautiful even without makeup."

Lucas laughs. "And at your age you shouldn't be eyeing the girls."

"I don't look at the girls in my class. They're stupid and ugly."

Agnes gets up. She climbs the stepladder to get a book. She is wearing a short skirt that reveals her garter belt and black stockings, which have a run in them. Noticing this, she wets her index finger and tries to stop the run with the saliva. To do this she must bend down, revealing white panties decorated with pink flowers—little girl's panties.

One evening, she stays until closing time. She says to Lucas, "I'll help you tidy up."

Lucas says, "Mathias does the tidying. He's good at it."

Mathias says to Agnes, "If you helped me I'd finish quicker, then I could make you some pancakes with jam, if you like them."

Agnes says, "Everybody likes pancakes with jam."

Lucas goes up to his room. A little while later, Mathias calls him. "It's ready, Lucas."

They eat pancakes with jam in the kitchen, they drink tea. Lucas doesn't speak. Agnes and Mathias laugh a lot. After the meal, Mathias says, "You'll have to walk Agnes home. It's dark outside."

Agnes says, "I can go on my own. I'm not afraid of the dark."

Lucas says, "Come on. I'll walk with you."

When they reach her house, Agnes asks, "Aren't you coming in?"

"No."

"Why not?"

"You're just a child, Agnes."

"No, I'm not a child anymore. I'm a woman. You wouldn't be the first to come into my bedroom. My parents aren't home. They're at work. Even if they were here . . . I have my own room and I can do what I like."

Lucas says, "Good night, Agnes. I have to go."

Agnes says, "I know where you're going. Down to that alley where the soldiers' girls are."

"That's right. But that's no concern of yours."

The next day, Lucas says to Mathias, "Before you invite someone to eat with us you should ask my opinion."

"Don't you like Agnes? Too bad. She's in love with you. It's obvious. It's because of you that she comes so often."

Lucas says, "You've got a fertile imagination, Mathias."

"Wouldn't you like to marry her?"

"Marry her? What an idea! No, certainly not."

"Why not? Are you still waiting for Yasmine? She won't come back."

Lucas says, "I don't want to marry anyone."

It is spring. The back door to the garden is open. Mathias is tending to his plants and his animals. He has a white rabbit, several cats, and the black dog that Joseph gave him. He is looking forward to the birth of some chicks being hatched out by a hen in the chicken coop.

Lucas is watching over the room where the children are bent over their books, absorbed in their reading.

A small boy raises his eyes, smiles at Lucas. He has blond hair, blue eyes. It's the first time he has been here. Lucas can't tear his eyes away from the child. He sits behind the counter, opens a book, and continues watching the unknown child. He feels a sudden, sharp pain in his left hand, which is resting on the book. A pair of compasses is stuck in the back of his hand. Half paralyzed by the intensity of the pain, Lucas turns slowly to Mathias.

"Why did you do that?"

Mathias hisses between his teeth, "I don't want you looking at him!"

"I wasn't looking at anyone."

"Yes you were! Don't lie to me! I saw you looking at him. I don't want you looking at him like that."

Lucas pulls out the compasses. He presses his handkerchief over the wound.

"I'm going upstairs to put some antiseptic on this."

When he comes back down the children have all gone. Mathias has pulled down the metal shutter in front of the door.

"I told them we were closing early today."

Lucas takes Mathias in his arms, carries him to the apartment, and puts him on the bed.

"What's the matter with you, Mathias?"

"Why were you looking at him, the blond boy?"

"He reminded me of someone."

"Someone you loved?"

"Yes. My brother."

"You mustn't love anyone else but me, not even your brother."

Lucas is silent.

Mathias continues, "There's no point in being intelligent. It's better to be beautiful and blond. If you got married, you could have children like him, the blond boy, like your brother. You'd have real children of your own, beautiful and blond, who aren't crippled. I'm not your son. I'm Yasmine's son."

Lucas says, "You are my son. I don't want any other children."

He shows Mathias his bandaged hand. "You hurt me, you know."

The child says, "And you hurt me, only you don't know it."

Lucas says, "I didn't want to hurt you. You must know one thing, Mathias: the only person in the world I care about is you."

The child says, "I don't believe you. Only Yasmine really loved me, and she's dead. I've told you that lots of times."

"Yasmine isn't dead. She just went away."

"She wouldn't have left without me, so she's dead." The child continues. "We must close down the reading room. What made you open a reading room in the first place?"

"I did it for you. I thought it would help you make friends."

"I don't want friends. I never asked you for a reading room. In fact, I'm asking you to close it."

Lucas says, "I'll close it. I'll tell the children tomorrow evening that the weather is nice enough to read and draw outside."

The little blond boy returns the next day. Lucas doesn't look at him. He stares at the lines, the letters in a book.

Mathias says, "You don't dare look at him. But you're dying to, all the same. You've been reading that page for the last five minutes."

Lucas closes the book and buries his face in his hands.

Agnes comes into the library. Mathias runs to meet her, she gives him a kiss. Mathias asks, "Why did you stop coming?"

"I haven't had time. I've been on a teacher training course in the next town. I wasn't home very often."

"But now you'll stay here, in our town?"

"Yes."

"Will you come and eat pancakes with us this evening?"

"I'd love to, but I have to look after my brother. Our parents are at work."

Mathias says, "Bring him with you, your little brother. There will be enough pancakes to eat. I'll go and make the batter."

"And I'll tidy up the shop for you."

Mathias goes up to the apartment. Lucas says to the children, "You can take the books that are out on the tables. The sheets of paper as well, and a box of colored pencils each. You shouldn't be cooped up in here in this weather. Go and read and draw in your gardens or in the park. If you need anything you can come and see me."

The children leave. Finally only the little blond boy is left, sitting quietly at his desk. Lucas asks him softly, "What about you? Aren't you going home?"

The child doesn't answer. Lucas turns to Agnes.

"I didn't know he was your brother. I knew nothing about him."

"He's shy. His name is Samuel. I suggested he come here, now that he's learning to read. He's the youngest. My brother Simon has been working at the factory for five years. He is a truck driver."

The blond child gets up and takes his sister's hand. "Are we going to eat pancakes with the man?"

Agnes says, "Yes, let's go up. Mathias will need some help."

They go up the stairs leading to the apartment. In the kitchen Mathias is mixing batter.

Agnes says, "Mathias, meet my little brother. He's called Samuel. I'm sure you'll be good friends. You're more or less the same age."

Mathias's eyes open wide, he drops the wooden spoon, he leaves the kitchen.

Agnes turns to Lucas. "What's wrong?"

Lucas says, "Mathias has probably gone to look for something in his room. Start cooking the pancakes, Agnes. I'll be back in a moment."

Lucas goes into Mathias's room. The child is lying on his eiderdown. He says, "Leave me alone. I want to sleep."

"You invited them, Mathias. It's bad manners."

"I invited Agnes. I didn't know he was her brother."

"I didn't know either. Make an effort for Agnes's sake, Mathias. You like Agnes, don't you?"

"And you like her brother. When I saw you all come into the kitchen I knew you were a real family. Beautiful, blond parents with their beautiful, blond child. I haven't got a family. I haven't got a mother or a father. I'm not blond. I'm ugly and crippled."

Lucas holds him tight. "Mathias, my little boy. You're my whole life."

Mathias smiles. “Fine. Let’s eat.”

In the kitchen the table is set, and there is a large pile of pancakes in the middle.

Agnes talks a lot, gets up frequently to serve the tea. She pays the same attention to her little brother as to Mathias.

“Jam? Cheese? Chocolate?”

Lucas watches Mathias. He eats little and never takes his eyes off the blond child. The blond child eats a lot. He smiles at Lucas when their eyes meet, he smiles at his sister when she hands him something; but when his blue eyes encounter Mathias’s dark stare, he lowers his gaze.

Agnes washes up with Mathias. Lucas goes to his room.

Mathias calls him later. “Time to walk Agnes and her brother home.”

Agnes says, “We’re really not afraid to walk home on our own.”

Mathias insists. “It’s good manners. Walk them home.”

Lucas walks them home. He bids them good night and goes to sit on the bench in the insomniac’s park.

The insomniac says, “It’s half past three. At eleven o’clock the child lit a fire in his room. I took the liberty of calling out to him, something I wouldn’t normally do. I was worried that he might set fire to something. I asked the child what he was doing, but he told me not to worry, he was just burning the rough notes from his homework in a metal pail in front of the window. I asked him why he didn’t use the stove to burn his papers. He said he didn’t want to go to the kitchen to do it. The fire went out shortly after, and I didn’t see the child or hear any sound after that.”

Lucas goes up the stairs, enters his room, then the child’s room. In front of the window there is a metal pail containing some burned paper. The child's bed is empty. On the pillow lies a blue notebook, closed. On the white label is written: MATHIAS'S NOTEBOOK. Lucas opens the notebook. There are only a few empty sheets and the edges of ripped-out pages. Lucas pulls open the dark red curtain. Alongside the skeleton of his mother and her baby hangs the little body of Mathias, already cold.

The insomniac hears a long scream. He goes down into the street, rings at Lucas's door. There is no reply. The old man goes up the stairs, enters Lucas's room, sees another door, opens it. Lucas is lying on the bed, clutching the child's body against his chest.

"Lucas?"

Lucas doesn't answer. His eyes stare wide open at the ceiling.

The insomniac goes back down into the street, he goes to call on Peter. Peter opens a window.

"What's going on, Michael?"

"Lucas needs you. Something terrible has happened. Come."

"Go home, Michael. I'll take care of everything."

He goes up to Lucas's apartment. He sees the metal pail, the two bodies stretched out on the bed. He pulls open the curtain, discovers the skeletons and, on the same hook, the end of a rope cut with a razor. He turns back to the bed, gently pushes the child's body away, and slaps Lucas on the face.

"Snap out of it!"

Lucas closes his eyes. Peter shakes him.

"Tell me what happened!"

Lucas says, "It's Yasmine. She's taken him from me."

Peter says firmly, "Don't ever say that again to anyone else but me, Lucas. Do you understand? Look at me!"

Lucas looks at Peter.

"Yes, I understand. What do I do now, Peter?"

"Nothing. Stay where you are. I'll bring you some tranquilizers. I'll take care of the formalities."

Lucas hugs Mathias's body.

"Thank you, Peter. I don't need any tranquilizers."

"No? Well, try to cry at least. Where are your keys?"

"I don't know. Maybe I left them in the front door."

"I'll lock up. You mustn't go out in this state. I'll be back."

Peter finds a bag in the kitchen, unhooks the skeletons, slips them into the bag, and takes them away with him.

Lucas and Peter walk behind Joseph's wagon, which is carrying the child's coffin.

At the cemetery a gravedigger sits on a mound of earth eating some bacon with onions.

Mathias is buried in the grave of Lucas's grandmother and grandfather.

When the gravedigger has filled in the hole, Lucas himself plants the cross, on which is engraved MATHIAS and two dates. The child lived seven years and four months.

Joseph asks, "Can I give you a lift, Lucas?"

Lucas says, "Go home, Joseph, and thank you. Thank you for everything."

"There's no point in staying here."

Peter says, "Come, Joseph. I'll go back with you."

Lucas hears the wagon depart. He sits down by the grave. The birds are singing.

A woman dressed in black comes by silently and places a bouquet of violets at the foot of the cross.

Later, Peter comes back. He touches Lucas on the shoulder.

"Come. It will soon be dark."

Lucas says, "I can't leave him here on his own at night. He's afraid of the dark. He's still so little."

"No, now he's not afraid anymore. Come, Lucas."

Lucas gets up, he stares at the grave. "I should have let him go with his mother. I made a fatal mistake, Peter, in wanting to keep the child at any price."

Peter says, "Every one of us commits a fatal mistake sometime in his life. When we realize it, the damage is already done."

They go back down into town. Outside the bookshop Peter asks, "Do you want to come to my place, or would you rather go in?"

"I'd rather go in."

Lucas goes in. He sits at his desk, looks at the closed door of the child's room, opens a school notebook, and writes, "Everything is fine with Mathias. He is always first at school, and he doesn't have nightmares anymore."

Lucas closes the notebook. He leaves the house, goes back to the cemetery, and sleeps on the child's grave.

At dawn, the insomniac comes to wake him.

"Come, Lucas. Time to open the bookshop."

"Yes, Michael."

8

Claus arrives by train. The little station hasn't changed, but there is now a bus for the passengers.

Claus doesn't take the bus. He goes on foot to the town center. The chestnut trees are in blossom; the street is as quiet and empty as it used to be.

Claus stops in the main square. There is a large three-story building in place of the simple, low houses. It is a hotel. Claus goes in and asks the receptionist, "When was this hotel built?"

"About ten years ago, sir. Would you like a room?"

"I don't know yet. I'll come back in a few hours. Could I leave my case here?"

"Please do."

Claus continues walking, he goes across town, passes the last of the houses, takes an unpaved road that leads to a playing field. Claus crosses the field and sits on the grass next to the river. Later, some children start playing ball. Claus asks one of them, "Has this playing field been here long?"

The child shrugs his shoulders. "The field? It's always been here."

Claus goes back to town. He goes up to the castle, then the cemetery. He searches for ages but can't find the grave of Grandmother and Grandfather. He goes back down into town. He sits on a bench in the main square. He watches the people doing their shopping, coming home from work, going for walks or bicycle rides. There are only a few cars. When the shops close, the square empties, and Claus goes back into the hotel.

"I'll take a room, please."

"For how many nights?"

"I don't know yet."

"Can I have your passport, sir?"

"Here."

"Are you a foreigner? Where did you learn to speak our language so well?"

"Here. I spent my childhood in this town."

She looks at him. "It must have been a long time ago."

Claus laughs. "Do I look that old?"

The young woman blushes. "No, no, I didn't mean that. I'll give you our best room, they're almost all empty. The season hasn't started yet."

"Do you get many tourists?"

"In summer, lots. I also recommend our restaurant, sir."

Claus goes up to his room on the second floor. Its two windows look out onto the square.

Claus eats in the deserted restaurant and goes back to his room. He opens his case, puts his clothes in the dresser, pulls up a chair to one of the windows, and looks out onto the empty street. On the other side of the square, the old houses have remained intact. They have been restored, repainted pink, yellow, blue, and green. The ground floor of each is occupied by a shop: a grocer, a souvenir shop, a dairy, a bookshop, a boutique. The bookshop is in the blue house where it used to be when Claus was a child and went there to buy paper and pencils.

The next day, Claus goes back to the playing field, the castle, the cemetery, the station. When he feels tired, he goes into a bar; he sits in a park. Later in the afternoon, he comes back to the main square. He goes into the bookshop.

A man with white hair sits at the counter, reading by the light of a desk lamp. The shop is in darkness. There are no customers. The white-haired man gets up.

"Excuse me, I forgot to turn on the lights."

The room and window lights come on. The man asks, "Can I help you?"

Claus says, "Please don't bother. I'm just looking."

The man takes off his glasses. "Lucas!"

Claus smiles. "You know my brother! Where is he?"

The man repeats, "Lucas!"

"I'm Lucas's brother. I'm called Claus."

"Don't joke, Lucas, please."

Claus takes his passport from his pocket. "See for yourself."

The man examines the passport. "That doesn't prove anything."

Claus says, "I'm sorry, I have no other means of proving my identity. I am Claus T. and I've come to look for my brother, Lucas. You know him. He has certainly told you about me, his brother Claus."

"Yes, he often talked to me about you, but I must admit I never believed you really existed."

Claus laughs. "Whenever I spoke to people about Lucas, they didn't believe me either. Rather funny, don't you think?"

"No, not really. Come, let's sit down over there."

He points to a low table and some armchairs at the back of the shop, in front of the French windows opening onto the garden.

"If you're not Lucas, I had better introduce myself. I am called Peter. Peter N. But if you aren't Lucas, why did you come here, to this particular place?"

Claus says, "I arrived yesterday. First I went to Grandmother's house, but it's no longer there. There's a playing field there instead. I came in here because this used to be a book and stationery shop when I was a child. We often came here to buy paper and pencils. I can still remember the man who ran it, a pale, fat man. I was hoping to find him here."

"Victor?"

"I don't know his name. I never did."

"He was called Victor. He's dead."

"Of course. He was getting on a bit even then."

"That's right."

Peter looks at the garden disappearing in the darkness.

Claus says, "I naively expected to find Lucas in Grandmother's house after all these years. Where is he?"

Peter continues looking out into the dark. "I don't know."

"Is there anyone in this town who might know?"

"No, I don't think so."

"Did you know him well?"

Peter looks Claus straight in the eyes. "As well as you can know anyone."

Peter leans across the table, grips Claus's shoulders. "Stop it,

Lucas, stop this play-acting! It's pointless! Aren't you ashamed to be doing this to me?"

Claus frees himself, gets up. "I can see you were very close, you and Lucas."

Peter falls back into his chair. "Yes, very. Forgive me, Claus. I knew Lucas when he was fifteen. At the age of thirty he disappeared."

"Disappeared? You mean he left this town?"

"The town and maybe even the country. Then he returns today with a different name. I always thought that play on words with your names was stupid."

"Our grandfather had that double name, Claus-Lucas. Our mother, who had a great deal of affection for her father, gave us these two names. It's not Lucas standing here before you, Peter, it's Claus."

Peter gets up. "Very well, Claus. In that case I must give you something that your brother Lucas left with me. Wait here."

Peter goes up to the apartment. He comes back shortly after with five large school notebooks.

"Here. These are meant for you. He had a lot more to start with, but he took them back, corrected them, erased everything that wasn't indispensable. If he'd had the time I think he would have eliminated everything."

Claus shakes his head. "No, not everything. He would have kept what was essential. For me."

He takes the notebooks, he smiles. "At last, here is the proof of Lucas's existence. Thank you, Peter. Has anyone read them?"

"Apart from me, no."

"I'm staying at the hotel across the way. I'll be back."

Claus reads all night, occasionally raising his eyes to look at the street.

Above the bookshop the light stays on for a long time in two of the three windows in the apartment. The third stays dark.

In the morning, Peter raises the metal shutter of the shop. Claus goes to bed. After noon, Claus leaves the hotel. He has a meal in one of the bars in town where they serve hot dishes all day.

The sky is overcast. Claus goes back to the playing field, sits next to the river. He stays there until night falls and it begins to rain. When Claus arrives back at the main square the bookshop is already closed. Claus rings at the front door of the apartment. Peter leans out of the window.

"The door is open. I was expecting you. Just come up."

Claus finds Peter in the kitchen. There are pans boiling on the stove.

Peter says, "The meal isn't ready yet. I've got some brandy. Would you like some?"

"Yes. I've read the notebooks. What happened afterward? After the death of the child?"

"Nothing. Lucas kept on working. He opened the shop in the morning, he closed it at night. He served his customers without saying a word. He hardly ever spoke. Some people thought he was mute. I often came to see him. We played chess in silence. He played badly. He didn't read or write anymore. I think he ate very little and hardly slept. The light was on all night in his room, but he wasn't in. He went walking in the dark streets of the town and in the cemetery. He said that the best place to sleep was the grave of someone you'd loved."

Peter is silent; he pours the drinks.

Claus says, "And then? Go on, Peter."

"Five years later, in the course of the work being done to lay out the playing field, I heard that the body of a woman had been discovered buried in the riverbank, near your grandmother's house. I told Lucas about it. He thanked me, and the next day he disappeared. No one has seen him since. On his desk he left a letter entrusting the house and the bookshop to me. The saddest thing about this story, you see, Claus, was that Yasmine's body was never identified. The authorities botched the whole affair. There are bodies in the ground everywhere in this unhappy land since the war and the revolution. This body could have been any woman who had tried to cross the border and stepped on a mine. Lucas wouldn't have been questioned."

Claus says, "He could come back now. There's the statute of limitations."

"Yes, I suppose so. After twenty years there is a statute of limitations." Peter looks Claus in the eyes. "That's right, Claus. Lucas could come back now."

Claus counters Peter's gaze. "Yes, Peter. Lucas will probably come back."

"They say that he's hiding in the forest and that he roams the streets of the town after dark. But that's just talk."

Peter shakes his head. "Come to my room, Claus. I'll show you Lucas's letter."

Claus reads: "I entrust the house and the bookshop that forms part of it to Peter N.—on the condition that he maintain the premises *in their present state*—until my return or, failing that, the return of my brother Claus T. Signed: Lucas T."

Peter says, "He underlined 'in their present state.' Now, whether you are Claus or Lucas, this house belongs to you."

"Listen, Peter, I'm only here for a short time, on a thirty-day visa. I'm a foreign citizen, and as you know, foreigners are not allowed to own any property here."

Peter says, "But you can accept the profits from the bookshop which I've been depositing in a bank every month for the last twenty years."

"What do you live on, then?"

"I have a government pension, and I rent out Victor's house. I only take care of the bookshop for you two. I keep careful accounts, you can check them."

Claus says, "Thank you, Peter. I don't need the money, and I don't wish to check the accounts. I came back only to see my brother."

"Why didn't you ever write to him?"

"We decided to separate. It had to be a total separation. The border wasn't enough. We needed silence as well."

"Yet you came back. Why?"

"The test has lasted long enough. I'm tired and ill. I want to see Lucas again."

"You know that you won't see him again."

A woman's voice calls from the next room.

"Is there someone there, Peter? Who is it?"

Claus looks at Peter. "You've got a wife? You're married?"

"No, it's Clara."

"Clara? She isn't dead?"

"We thought she was, yes. But she was just in prison. Shortly after Lucas disappeared she came back. She had no job and no money. She was looking for Lucas. I let her stay at my place, that is, here. She has the small room, the child's room. I take care of her. Do you want to see her?"

"Yes, I'd like to see her."

Peter opens the door of the room.

"Clara, a friend has come to see us."

Claus goes into the room. Clara is sitting in a rocking chair in front of the window, with a blanket over her knees and a shawl around her shoulders. She is holding a book, but she's not reading it. She is staring into space through the gap in the window. She is rocking.

Claus says, "Hello, Clara."

Clara doesn't look at him; she recites in a monotonous voice, "It's raining as usual. Fine, cold rain, falling on the houses, the trees, the graves. When they come to see me the rain trickles over their distorted faces. They look at me and the cold grows more intense. My walls no longer protect me. They never protected me. Their solidity is mere illusion, their whiteness is stained."

Her voice changes suddenly. "I'm hungry, Peter! When do we eat? With you the meals are always late."

Peter returns to the kitchen.

Claus says, "It's me, Clara."

"You?"

She looks at Claus, holds out her arms to him. He kneels down at her feet, rests his head on her knees. Clara strokes his hair. Claus takes Clara's hand, presses it against his cheek, against his lips. A thin, wizened hand, covered with the marks of old age.

She says, "You left me alone for a long time, too long, Thomas."

Tears run down her face. Claus wipes them away with his handkerchief.

"I'm not Thomas. Have you no memory of Lucas?"

Clara closes her eyes, shakes her head, "You haven't changed, Thomas. You've aged a little, but you are still the same. Kiss me."

She smiles, revealing her toothless gums.

Claus draws back, stands up. He goes to the window, looks out to the street. The main square is empty and dark in the rain. Only the lighted entrance of the hotel is visible in the dark.

Clara starts rocking again. "Go away. Who are you? What are you doing in my room? Why doesn't Peter come? I want to eat and go to bed. It's late."

Claus leaves Clara's room, he finds Peter in the kitchen. "Clara is hungry."

Peter carries a tray in to Clara. When he comes back he says, "She likes her food. I take her a tray three times a day. Fortunately, she sleeps a lot because of her medication."

"She must be a burden to you."

Peter serves up stew with some pasta. "No, not really. She doesn't bother me. She treats me as if I were her valet, but I don't mind. Eat up, Claus."

"I'm not hungry. Does she ever go out?"

"Clara? No. She doesn't like to, and in any case she would just get lost. She reads a lot and likes looking at the sky."

"What about the insomniac? His house must have been opposite, there where the hotel is now."

Peter gets up. "Yes, that's right. I'm not hungry either. Come, let's go out."

They walk down the street. Peter points out a house. "That's where I lived at that time. On the second floor. If you're not too tired, I can show you where Clara used to live."

"I'm not tired."

Peter stops in front of a two-story building on Station Road.

"This is it. This house will soon be demolished, like nearly all the houses on this street. They are too old and unsanitary."

Claus shivers. "Let's go back. I'm frozen."

They part in front of the hotel entrance. Claus says, "I've been to the cemetery several times, but I can't find Grandmother's grave."

"I'll show you tomorrow. Come to the bookshop at six o'clock. It will still be light."

In an abandoned part of the cemetery, Peter sticks his umbrella in the ground.

"Here's the grave."

"How can you be so sure? There's nothing here but weeds. No cross, nothing. You could be mistaken."

"Mistaken? If only you knew how many times I came here looking for your brother Lucas. Even afterward, later, when he was no longer here. This spot has been the end of an almost daily walk for me."

They go back into town. Peter attends to Clara, then they drink brandy in what used to be Lucas's room. The rain falls on the windowsill, drips into the room. Peter goes to get a cloth to mop up the water.

"Tell me about yourself, Claus."

"There's nothing to tell."

"Over there, is life easier?"

Claus shrugs his shoulders. "It's a society based on money. There is no place for questions about life. I've spent thirty years in mortal solitude."

"Did you never have a wife, a child?"

Claus laughs. "Women, yes. Lots of women. No children."

After a silence he asks, "What did you do with the skeletons, Peter?"

"I put them back in their place. Do you want to see them?"

"We mustn't disturb Clara."

"We don't need to cross the room. There's another door. Don't you remember?"

"How could I remember?"

"You might have noticed as you went past. It's the first door on the left as you come to the landing."

"No, I didn't notice."

"The door does blend in with the wallpaper."

They enter a small space separated from Clara's room by a thick curtain. Peter switches on a flashlight, illuminating the skeletons.

Claus whispers, "There are three of them."

Peter says, "You don't need to whisper. Clara won't wake up. She takes strong sedatives. I forgot to tell you that Lucas dug up Mathias's body two years after the burial. He told me that it was easier for him, he was tired of spending his nights at the cemetery to keep the child company."

Peter shines the flashlight on a mattress beneath the skeletons.

"That's where he slept."

Claus touches the mattress, the gray army blanket that covers it.

"It's warm."

"What's on your mind, Claus?"

"I'd like to sleep here, just for one night. Do you mind, Peter?"

"This is your home."

Report drawn up by the authorities of the town of K. for the attention of the embassy of D.

Re: request for the repatriation of your citizen Claus T., presently held in the prison of the town of K.

Claus T., aged fifty, holder of a valid passport and a thirty-day tourist visa, arrived in this town on April 2 of this year. He rented a room in the only hotel in town, the Grand Hotel in the main square.

Claus T. spent three weeks in the hotel, behaving like a tourist, walking around town, visiting historic sights, having his meals in the hotel restaurant, or in other restaurants in town.

Claus T. often visited the bookshop opposite the hotel to buy paper and pencils. Conversant in the local language, he chatted readily with the bookseller, Mrs. B., and with other persons in public places.

After three weeks, Claus T. asked Mrs. B. if she would rent

him the two rooms above the bookshop on a monthly basis. As he offered a good price, Mrs. B. gave up the two-room apartment and went to stay with her daughter, who lives nearby.

Claus T. requested an extension to his visa on three occasions, which was granted without difficulty. However, his fourth request for an extension was refused in August. Claus T. disregarded this refusal, and owing to negligence on the part of our employees, the matter rested there until the month of October. On October 30, in the course of a routine identity check, our local police established that Claus T.'s papers were no longer in order.

At this point, Claus T. had run out of money. He owed two months' rent to Mrs. B. He was hardly eating. He went from bar to bar playing the harmonica. Drunkards bought him drinks. Mrs. B. brought him a little soup each day.

During his interrogation, Claus T. claimed to have been born in our country, and to have spent his childhood in our town, at his grandmother's house, and declared his wish to remain here until the return of his brother Lucas T. The said Lucas does not appear in any of the records of the town of K. Neither does Claus T.

We request you to settle the enclosed invoice (fine, administrative costs, rent for Mrs. B.) and to repatriate Claus T. on your own responsibility.

Signed, on behalf of the authorities of the town of K.: I.S.

Postscript

We have naturally, for reasons of security, examined the manuscript in the possession of Claus T. He claims that this manuscript proves the existence of his brother Lucas, who wrote the major part of it himself, Claus himself having merely added the last few pages, chapter number eight. However, the manuscript is in the same handwriting from beginning to end, and the sheets of paper show no signs of age. The entire text was written in one sequence, by the same person, over a period of time not exceeding six months, that is, by Claus T. himself during his stay in our town.

As for the content of the text, this can only be a fiction, since neither the events described nor the characters portrayed ever existed in the town of K., with the sole exception of one person, the supposed grandmother of Claus T., whom we have traced. This woman did in fact own a house on the present site of our playing field. Deceased without heir thirty-five years ago, she appears in our records under the name Maria Z., wife of V.

It is possible that during the war she was entrusted with the care of one or more children.